The
Pleasure
is all Mine

By the same author

Dark Temptation: The Naughty Proposal!

The Pleasure is all Mine

Shanaya Taneja

Srishti
PUBLISHERS & DISTRIBUTORS

SRISHTI PUBLISHERS & DISTRIBUTORS
Registered Office: N-16, C.R. Park
New Delhi – 110 019
Corporate Office: 212A, Peacock Lane
Shahpur Jat, New Delhi – 110 049
editorial@srishtipublishers.com

First published by
Srishti Publishers & Distributors in 2016

10 9 8 7 6 5 4 3 2 1

This is a work of fiction. The characters, places, organisations and events described in this book are either a work of the author's imagination or have been used fictitiously. Any resemblance to people, living or dead, places, events, communities or organisations is purely coincidental.

Dedicated to
all my past, present and future lovers.

Sanjay woke up first. Perhaps because of the warm breasts pressed against his chest, or the round buttock beneath his hand. Trisha's long dark hair was spread on the bed; her skin was warm and smelled of their lovemaking. She burrowed closer in her sleep, and his body responded.

He loved to watch her wake up. It made waiting for her on the bedside such a pleasant exercise in anticipation.

Trisha was a very beautiful girl. Her long, shiny black hair fell thickly around her face; her thin black eyebrows accentuated her hazel eyes. The face was a sculptor's dream, with a small nose and luscious lips. She wore no makeup and no clothes, covered by only a thin baby pink silk sheet.

Her eyes opened sensuously to the feel of Sanjay's fingers on her cheek, his voice caressing her. She sighed and leaned closer as he placed a kiss on her forehead. Butterflies immediately came alive in her stomach, dancing and jumping like crazy.

"Wake up, Trisha."

Trisha opened her heavy eyes with a yawn. The bright lights of the room burned her eyes. "Mmm," she murmured. Burying her face in the crook of his neck, she pressed herself more tightly against him. Sanjay leaned over again to drop a kiss on the top of her head.

She tugged on his elbow, pulling him closer. He stiffened as the heat from her body seeped into his. He inhaled her scent and fought the urge to breathe deeper. Never in his life had someone rendered him speechless with just a look. They continued to stare at one another, at a deadlock, when suddenly he grinned, and she got a tingle in her stomach. His gaze wandered down her neck, to her breasts – her impressive breasts, which swelled under his gaze.

Sanjay came closer, his lips brushing Trisha's tenderly, yet teasingly. The same jolt of electricity that he always felt ran through his veins. If he'd been standing, it would have brought him to his knees. He loved kissing her. He actually loved everything about her. His thumb rubbed against her cheek as his lips continued to sip at hers. She returned his soft butterfly kisses, her sighs becoming lost in his mouth as he deepened it. He pulled away, his lips remaining a hairbreadth from hers as they spread into a smile. The back of his fingers brushed along her cheek, her skin smooth and silky under his touch. His eyes stared into hers, passion deepening the pupils. "I am addicted to you, Trisha." The scent of the champagne they'd been drinking last night wafted across her nose.

He captured her lips in another slow kiss, their tongues battling and teasing each other. God, he loved the way she kissed, the way her lips moulded to his.

He had no need to take permission to tease her lips apart. He liked to have her at his convenience. The roughness of his unshaven chin against her face, the deep probing explorations of his tongue, the erotic movements of his powerful and knowing fingers at her ears, the heavy textured weight of his chest against her breasts – all came together to overpower her defenses.

This wasn't a first for him. He had never had a problem in getting a girl, and for him, they were a mere means to satisfy his insatiable urges. He ran an advertising production company where many aspiring girls flocked with a dream to become a star. He dated a few, slept with many, but respected none. They were toys of sensual satisfaction. He was never serious about any of them. Sanjay's eyes glittered with open amusement at this indisputable evidence that he had an upper hand with girls. A power many men would kill to get. Most models that came to him had great bodies, and that was what he loved. He loved being in bed with them, but had never gotten attached to any girl. Not even his wife.

For a moment, he wondered why he liked being with Trisha so much. It wasn't just the physical attraction, he knew. It was something else. Something he couldn't quite put his finger on.

Sanjay moved up to grab a cigarette. He eyed her and wondered why she was looking up at him like that. She appeared amused. Like she had some private joke she was bursting to share.

Trisha looked up at the ceiling as she remembered her past in Surajpur. She was born in this small town in the Mandi district of Himachal Pradesh. When she started off, she had no judgment when it came to men. Plus, Trisha always opened her heart when she opened her legs. She just had this regrettable inclination to fall for guys too soon, long before she knew their flaws or had any rationale to trust them. Unlike most women who indulged in one-night stands merely because they loved sex, Trisha had them because she loved men. Three drinks and three hours with some dark-eyed handsome stranger, and she was ready to be his good-time girl for the long haul. Until she woke up the next morning and discovered his apartment smelled like dog poop and there were leftovers of last week's pizza on the floor.

In the two years since she had come to Mumbai, Trisha had practically lived at a single room apartment, working for pennies and burning through the little savings she had. Her only goal was to transform her passion for acting into employment as an actor. She had the skills, but she lacked the credentials to get hired by traditional means. She needed to get in through the back door.

That's when she decided to meet the right men. Men who would help her achieve her goals.

"You know Sanjay, when I was seventeen, I was so absolutely incredible that my own father didn't want to let me out on my own. He felt I was bound to have affairs with every guy in the street or something like that." She pursed her lips.

At seventeen, tall but curvy at the right places, she had developed her height and shape well in time to be a model. She was blessed with a beautiful body. She had soon learned to hide her miseries behind a prickly aggressive tongue that could do much more than she could have ever imagined. She wanted to be rich, but saw no hope in her mother's eyes to ease her through a painful poverty. Though her mother was warm and loving, she had not understood all her needs. Nor had her father.

Sanjay sat at the corner of the bed. He was forty, but looked pretty young for his age. He had black, straight hair, and a well-chiselled jaw line. He enjoyed a great deal of success with the opposite sex because of his looks, as also his advertising business.

"So I left home to pursue my dream of becoming an actress," continued Trisha. "I mean, I had to come to Mumbai and follow my dreams. It would have been impossible in a small town like Surajpur." She sighed and wriggled around under the sheet. "Can you pass me a cigarette, please?"

Sanjay picked a packet of Marlboro from the side table and handed one to her. She lit the cigarette and took a long drag. "Want to hear more about my grey past?"

One corner of his lips twitched at her question. "I want to know everything about you, Trisha."

She smiled. "You're so adorable baby. I liked you the moment I saw you. I'm crazy about you!" She moved over to where he was sitting. The silk sheet was left behind as she wound her arms around his neck and started to bite his ear. She had quite an incredible body, and Sanjay could not overlook that for her story.

"Want to go for another round?" Sanjay raised his eyes to her and smiled slightly.

She scrunched her nose up at his back.

"I saw that," he said, with a touch of scorn in his voice.

With the swiftness of a wild deer, she jumped off the bed and ran to the bathroom. "You have too much energy baby," she said, "but not now. We can do it again soon, but I need to relax a bit." She laughed. "I'm going to take a shower, then maybe we can get some dinner, and then we can come back and make it an all-night-long event!"

She vanished through the door and twisted the knob of the shower. As the first few drops of the warm water kissed her scintillating skin, she thought about Sanjay.

A month ago, she was having a particularly tough day; such where everything that could go wrong, went wrong. Her agent had fixed her appointments with some production houses so that she could try to get some work as an actress in advertisements. The last of her appointments was with a producer who had called her to a bar instead of the office. He had said that he was busy all day and the only time he could give her was in the night when he was out drinking with his friends. Trisha knew what that meant, but she was desperate for a role.

She had just entered the bar when the producer spotted her. She was wearing a figure-hugging black dress on her extremely fair body. Her hair was piled high on her head and she was carrying a matching black clutch bag. She knew she looked stunning. But to her surprise, the producer had called in another model too. So it was a battle of the hottest! She was ready for any challenge. She had been struggling for almost two years in Mumbai, and she had to end the dry spell.

A few drinks down and many accidental stokes to the producer's body later, she still hadn't won the role as he was more inclined towards the other girl. She looked at her...plastic beauty, like a doll. She seemed to be more fabricated than the cocktail she was drinking. It seemed as if each of her body part had been sculpted specially for display. She had huge breasts, emphasized by the skimpy red-coloured dress she was wearing.

Trisha looked into the eyes of the producer and could see him fucking the other girl right there. Judging by the flare of heat in the girl's eyes, she gauged she would be an easy and willing victim. Trisha had gone to the restroom to check on her make-up. While walking back, she bumped into a man and his drink got spilled over his clothes.

"Oh I am sorry, I didn't mean to—"

He looked at her and was probably mesmerized by her beauty. The frown on his face changed into a smile.

"It's ok. It's a minor accident, I guess," he said, trying to wipe away the whisky from his shirt.

"But I am sorry I spilled your drink. I can't get you a shirt right now, but can I buy you a drink?"

"I haven't heard a girl saying that line in years. I thought it was a guy's duty to say that."

"Well yes, men have the privilege to act chivalrous and I am sure every girl would like that. But in this case, I just want to make up for what I did."

"Sure, let's have a drink," he replied with a grin on his face.

The man introduced himself as Sanjay. They had a quick drink together and Trisha returned to the producer and the big-breast-girl.

For two more hours, she tried to lure the producer, but all in vain. So she left the bar and walked out in search of a cab. It was late at night and the only sound that could be heard was the echoing clomps of her heels down the footpath and the buzz of the fluorescent lights.

Trisha waited for the cab, staring at her shoes and trying to breathe herself calm. A black and clawing loneliness had crept into her bones, eating the marrow and leaving behind an ache she didn't know what to do with. Many kilometres away from anything resembling a home, she was in tears, bleary and tired and fuzzy. That's when she spotted Sanjay's face.

"Hello, we meet again. What a coincidence!" she said, a soft smile tugging at her lips.

They talked for a few minutes and when there was nothing much left to say, Sanjay suggested dinner. Trisha loved the idea and accepted it graciously.

They went to Aurus, a warm Italian restaurant in Juhu, where Sanjay knew he was unlikely to be spotted by any of his or his wife Bharti's friends. He called Bharti on the phone and made his excuses. They chatted over drinks where Trisha came to know that Sanjay was a producer of advertising films. He had built his company Brandwagon from scratch. He was looking for a fresh face for one of his clients, Lasense lingerie. He wanted someone pure, with natural beauty.

They ate ravioli and ordered the restaurant's most famous dish named Dark Temptations which had an assortment of chocolate and strawberries, so sinful that they couldn't have enough of it. Sanjay suggested that they have some more of it at his flat close by, and that's where it all began.

And yes, of course, she got the role in the Lasense advertisement, as the very next morning, Sanjay fixed her appointment with his *director Manoj Bhatt. While she had done a few small-time shoots for print advertisements and hoardings, this was her first step into television advertising, eventually kick-starting her career.*

Suddenly Trisha heard the bathroom door open, breaking her chain of thoughts. Sanjay was peeking in through the door. Trisha wrapped her hair in a white towel, and wore a small, white satin robe.

"I was waiting for you outside?"

She placed her hand on her hip as she tilted her head to the side, smiling at him. "And I was waiting for you inside," she said stepping out.

Sanjay eyed her satin-covered body, her bare thighs peeking out from under her robe. He wondered what she was wearing underneath the robe. Nothing whatsoever. His heart skipped a beat. He stood, and her eyes widened slightly in nervousness as he slowly strolled around her, never taking his gaze off her. She moved back a few steps until her back hit the wall. In a show of acceptance, she raised her chin, staring at him with a naughty smile. He braced his hands against the wall and leaned in close. Her whole body tingled in a way that made her weak. Her robe rubbed her breasts, and she struggled against the desire to arch her back and press herself into his chest. Their lips were so close she could smell the drink he'd had on his breath. All it would take to part hers would be a slight flick of his tongue. His eyes moved to her mouth, and she swallowed down a moan. He drove his tongue inside, and Trisha could do nothing more than respond. His kiss was wild, making her feel drunk and reckless. His manhood pressed against her.

"I want you right now Trisha."

"Come on Sanjay! You promised we'd go out for a lovely dinner. Let's do it tonight after dinner so that we can make it a night-long party." She tempted him. "Just like our first time!"

"Oh, yeah! Just like our first time, when you chose me." His smug response came out a little too soon.

"It's so not true!" she objected. "You are the one who smiled at me even though your drink got spilled on your shirt because of me. Now don't lie. You wanted me as soon as you saw me!"

Sanjay ran his hands on her flat stomach. She shivered. Trisha's phone rang. "Saved by the phone call!" She laughed, and walked over to answer it.

Sanjay fixed his pants, grabbed his shirt and buttoned it up.

"I have some good news for you Trisha," the manager from the agency told her over phone.

"What?"

"You remember I submitted your portfolio to Abhinav Deo?"

"Yes, I do."

"He has shortlisted you for casting in his movie and an interview has been scheduled for the same."

"What are you saying!" Trisha jumped up to do a victory dance, but then simmered down as she saw Sanjay staring at her.

"So look your most beautiful, Trisha! This could be very lucrative for both of us. I hear that each year he personally picks the model he wants to use."

"Wants to use?" Trisha weighed the question for a moment.

"Yes, you heard it right! He usually ends up dating his model – or even two as the grapevine goes – so you need to handle your obsessive-good-for-nothing-boyfriend Sanjay."

"Please don't say that."

"Oh, I will. You know, I got Sanjay the best models last year and worked my ass off for him, but that bastard has not even paid my commission for the same yet."

"Really?"

"I don't understand how you can tolerate him. No one in the industry likes him, and I am telling you he can just give you a role in three or four advertisements in an year. What you need is a movie! So it would be great if you could manage him and take out time for this interview," the manager said.

"I am not sure how I will manage that." She eyed Sanjay as she walked away from him to ensure he couldn't listen to the manager's voice."

"You can handle him," came the cheerful answer, showing more confidence than Trisha herself felt. "And some girls think that getting a meeting with Abhinav Deo is as good as getting to heaven, you know. He's very successful in the industry and quite a charmer, I hear. He can make your career!"

"I'm sure with success on his side as a director, he's had plenty of opportunities to practice his charms. A new one every day," she whispered into the phone.

"Well, that's not for me to keep track of. I am *your* manager. Now, can I confirm this interview?"

"Yes! I'll definitely go for it. Promise."

"But I won't promise you'll be offered the role," returned the manager. "My job was to get you the opportunity, now it's on you how you make the best use of it."

"I will try my best. Thanks a lot. Bye."

She hung up to face the impatient Sanjay waiting with his line of rapid fire questions.

"Who was it?" he asked suspiciously.

"Oh, it was the manager from my agency," she said vaguely.

"What did he say that you started jumping in excitement?"

"It's some breathtaking news. You've got to hear it Sanjay! I have an interview with Abhinav Deo tomorrow. You know, he is the guy who has been the number one director of advertising films for the longest time. But now he is directing a movie and is looking for a youthful and fresh face to star in it. I'm so excited to see him tomorrow night. Isn't that thrilling?"

Sanjay's eyes flared with anger and he turned to stare at her. He wasn't pleased at all. He had a grey past with Abhinav Deo and was shocked that he had come back to ruin his life. "What? Abhinav Deo? That prick!" His tone was high, vigorous, and in the very shrillness of his voice, there was an implicit warning for Trisha.

Trisha swallowed hard. "Why are you calling him a prick?" she asked with a lightness she did not feel.

"I don't think you need to know that!" came the derisive answer.

Trisha felt her insides curdling and took a tighter grip on her mobile phone to steady herself.

"That excuse for a human being who's known for playing around with girls' careers?" Sanjay chuckled, not too pleasantly. "He can't have you. You are mine. Just mine."

To help her through the awkward moment, Trisha laughed, a trilling little laugh that was pure nerves. The silence in the room was so long, so laden, that Trisha finally said, with another bright manufactured laugh, "Sanjay, I am not your slave. I can choose to make my own decisions."

"No!" Sanjay growled in warning.

She quietly studied him for a moment, his black eyes staring into hers. Trisha saw the anger in his eyes. "Then tell me what the real issue is. I sense something more than jealousy here?" Trisha controlled her temper. Till she got any other modelling assignment, Sanjay was her only hope.

Sanjay looked down for a moment and intertwined his fingers. There was a short heavy silence. "You are a stubborn woman." Sanjay snarled, his voice measured but coolly insulting.

Choosing to ignore his threatening tone, Trisha glanced down at her slender tapered fingers with their polished pink nails, but other than that, her expression remained totally serene. When she looked up again, she smiled composedly, "That I am."

"Okay, I will tell you," he said at last, his voice now no longer scornful, but cold and controlled. He glanced at her through his lashes, then took a deep breath. Sanjay appeared to go pale right before her eyes. "Abhinav and I were partners in a production company which produced the best advertising films of the country. Apart from being business partners, we were very good friends too. We used to work late nights to make our company profitable and keep our clients happy."

Trisha's eyebrow rose in interest. "Then?"

"Abhinav was over ambitious. Once we became a large company, he started having arguments with me over the profit sharing. He said he was the one who got most of the clients and so he wanted more share in the profits."

"Well, that sounds pretty logical. Did you give him an extra share?"

His shrewd eyes narrowed slightly and he laughed nastily. "You are too innocent, Trisha. You do not understand business. That's why I didn't want to tell you in the first place," he said stiffly.

Trisha's heart did a quick flop, then righted itself at once when she heard him treat her like a stupid person. "I hate it when you treat me like a fool. I understand everything," she sneered, her eyes narrowing at him. "Tell me if you want to, else I am not interested in your stupid story." She rose up from the bed instantly. Her gaze shot back to his and she watched him in silence.

She noticed a muscle tense in his cheek. Sanjay watched her, lost in his thoughts about how to handle this. If it would have been some other girl, he would have slapped her and asked her to get lost. He had done that in the past. Models had been nothing but his playthings. But this was different. He felt strongly possessive about Trisha. He wasn't sure what this was, but didn't want to lose what he had with Trisha. He would give anything if she would talk properly to him, trust him, but he knew that would be asking for a miracle.

Trisha opened her mouth to voice the remaining grudges in her heart, but suddenly she found herself sick and tired of the meaningless exchange.

Seconds of silence ticked by, and Trisha thought her heart would scream from inquisitiveness. She had to know what Sanjay was thinking. Raising her eyes, she stared into Sanjay's concerned ones.

Sanjay stood up and placed his hands on her shoulders. "Calm down, I didn't mean to offend you. And sit, I want to tell you everything," he murmured close to her face.

Her lips thinned into a tight line. She was angry and had every right to be. What the hell had gotten into him? She crossed her arms and eyed him suspiciously.

Sanjay cleared his throat, getting her attention. "While Abhinav got in more clients, I was more creative than him. And I worked late nights to create great films which made us popular in the industry. Our popularity grew and we started getting much larger clients."

She glanced at Sanjay and narrowed her eyes, his words finally sinking in. "Hmm. Ok," Trisha said softly.

"I sensed that Abhinav was not satisfied and he would soon cut himself off the company. So I started embezzling funds from the production budgets as that was directly under my supervision. I wanted to be sure that the bastard got nothing out of this deal as the embezzled money wouldn't show up during the split. I was the king of the advertising industry and couldn't let a peasant like him come in my way." He said stiffly, as he went and punched the wall to vent out his anger.

"You are a shrewd businessman, Sanjay." She shook her head with an exasperated sigh. "This story tells me that you are the one who stole money from him and not Abhinav," she said, trying to take her mind off her twisting emotions.

"Yes, I did. What's wrong with that?"

Trisha heard him laugh again, this time quite nastily.

"It wasn't his money anyway." Sanjay scowled.

"Why do you say so?" Trisha stared at him with widening eyes.

"When I wanted to start the company, my father-in-law funded the entire business for us. Then we both worked hard for years to make it the number one company in the industry. And just at that point, he decided to quit. If I had a gun I would have shot him dead," he said angrily. "Now do you get what I am saying?"

Trisha stared at him with a pointed look. "You married a girl with a rich father and used that money to set up a company. Then you used a creative man to help your company grow to a certain level and then you literally kicked him out of business. If you can do all that to make your career, then that makes the two of us."

"What do you mean?" Sanjay's brow creased.

She crossed her arms and eyed him guardedly. "I appreciate that you wanted to tell me everything. And actually it further motivates me to do anything and everything to make my career. That's what you have done. Now don't be a hypocrite and let me do what I want to do," she replied smartly, turning her nose up to appear snobbish.

"You are not going to meet that jerk! Do you understand that?" Sanjay narrowed his eyes at her in censure.

A worried frown marred her delicate features. "Stop shouting at me! I am not your wife. I am a free bird and have come to

Mumbai to make my career and not sit at home and make food for you. I will go and meet him," Trisha yelled in a firm voice.

She marched crossly to the dressing table and fussily started to apply her makeup. She brushed her hair from her face with a sigh.

Sanjay opened his mouth to speak, then changed his mind, his mouth clamping closed with a frown.

"Ok, I'm sorry. I just don't know why you want this stupid career of yours. Why don't you—"

"Why don't I...what?" she interrupted callously. "Leave my career and get married to you? And what do you propose we do with your failing marriage and your wife? And what do we do about your debts? You are up to your nose in debts. You think you will be able to afford me?"

Sanjay continued in a forcibly controlled tone. "I can afford you forever. The company is in debts, not me. I told you I had embezzled a lot of funds and all of it is stashed as diamonds with me. I can make a sale and we can create a future if you want," Sanjay said in an emphatic tone.

"Oh, gee," Trisha snapped with sarcasm. "That makes me feel much better. This whole situation might not bother you, but it scares the hell out of me."

"But—" Sanjay's eyebrow rose a fraction.

"Look, sweety," her voice softened, "I don't interfere in your professional or personal life, so I expect the same from you. I am not looking for any future or any sort of bindings or commitments. I believe in *now*, and right now, I am hungry." She looked into the mirror and applied mascara.

She got up and placed her hand on his arm, making him turn to look at her. "Sanjay, can you act normal now and not like a bossy husband? Can we have a good evening and not fight like a married couple? Let's go out for dinner, just like we planned."

Trisha glanced up at him and didn't miss the frown that suddenly creased his brow.

Wrestling with mixed emotions, Sanjay tried to control his anger; he didn't want to sleep alone tonight. He took her hands in his and brought them to his mouth, his lips softly kissing the knuckles of each hand. "Sure, let's go."

Sanjay helped her in his Jaguar and settled her into the luscious leather seats.

He decided the restaurant, which she hated, but she was happy that he didn't take him to the place she actually loved. She didn't want his presence to taint the places she really liked.

Once at the exclusive restaurant, they wove through the other diners. A few stopped chewing and stared at him distastefully as he passed them by, but most of them ignored him.

"You are very beautiful," he said as he gazed at her over the menu once seated.

She gave him a faint, shy smile. "So are you."

That made him smile.

"You are looking gorgeous in this black dress," he remarked approvingly, his darkened eyes travelling slowly over the smooth curves of her breasts down over an expanse of luscious skin on her legs. She had chosen to wear the dress against her better judgment, yet now, with his gaze sweeping down to the shadowed cleft between her breasts, she felt undressed, loving her choice.

"And you did very well, too, in your ten minutes," she said, prodding at a fork, but seeing him beyond it – well-knit, immeasurably masculine and immaculate in a blue dinner jacket.

"Oh, I think you took much longer than ten minutes to do your makeup," he taunted returning to his natural self.

The waiter arrived and looked up in anticipation. "Good evening. Are you ready with the order?"

"Who called you? Did you hear me call for a waiter? Don't you see we are having a bit of private time here?" Sanjay frowned deeply.

"I am sorry sir—"

"It's okay," Trisha intervened, simultaneously pressing her toes on Sanjay's manhood from under the table. She knew how to control this mad horse. She eyed Sanjay and smiled at him.

He looked at her as a silent moan tried to slip past his lips, which he hid behind a fake cough.

Trisha looked through the menu quickly. "Please get us Chateau St. Michelle red wine first." The waiter rushed away to avoid any further embarrassment.

Sanjay couldn't wait and slid in across from her and ordered the waitress who was passing by to the other table to get two asparagus salads.

"Of course," the waitress gushed. She didn't even look at them and quickly disappeared.

Trisha smoothed the white table cloth under her hands as the waitress ran off to the kitchen. "I am not sure if I will like asparagus salad."

"You will like this one. Trust me. I know what I am ordering," he said. "It's delicious."

Trisha watched as he shook out his napkin and laid it in his lap. She followed suite and laid out the napkin on her black dress.

Trisha was disappointed when the salad came in. She was annoyed to discover that it was a single piece of asparagus on a leaf of lettuce, artistically arranged and drizzled with some kind of herbs that stung her nose all the way from the table. A lone slice of onion peeked from beneath the lettuce. She snatched the menu from Sanjay and decided to order the remaining dishes. Sanjay didn't create a scene as he was getting a foot massage from her toes. She knew how to manage him, after all.

The waiter brought the red wine and Sanjay poured it for them, toasting the beginning of what he hoped would be a mutually satisfying night as he looked down at her beautiful toes fighting against the wall of his trousers.

He dipped his fingers in the wine and brushed her lips with them. She shyly licked them, her anticipation mounting. Then she sucked them hard, and that sensual, knowing look flashed in his dark eyes again as she pressed his manhood real hard with her foot.

He wanted her. She knew that. This was the moment for her as well. Her body was open and creamy for him, and if he touched her, she thought she would just clot and pour into his hands. He studied her from across the table. The blue light of the bar cast an otherworldly glow over her fair skin. She was an attractive girl, small and lovely and full of terrible power beyond his knowledge. He looked Trisha over, head to toe. Her short skirt. Shiny heels. Her luscious legs, sexy as hell. He was crazy about her.

She sipped her obscenely expensive red wine with relish and smiled at Sanjay. She was a charming girl. He had had various affairs outside marriage, but this was different; this time, for the first time, he wished he was free from his marriage.

"I met this man once who made me promises of Louis Vuitton clothes, a Jaguar car and a bungalow," said Trisha. "But our affair didn't last for more than three weeks. Isn't that funny?"

Sanjay didn't find it funny. He wondered why she had thought of mentioning that now.

After dinner, Sanjay cleared the bill and she snuggled up closer to him as they walked to the car. "Let's go back and have our night long private party," she said, her lips spreading into a smile.

He turned to her with eyes full of emotions. Jumbled emotions that mirrored her own. "Let's go home." He pointed to his car. "Get in."

Home! Was she really going home? she wondered. Thanks to Sanjay, she had got a role in a TV advertisement. She wished she could tell her father. Would he be proud? It was hard for her to even imagine pride on her father's face. In its place, there had always been worry. Judgment. Exasperation. And Trisha had deserved that. She'd been a rotten daughter, at least from the time she was fourteen or so. After her mother died, she'd gone bad, and she'd stayed that way right up to now. As a teenager, Trisha had accepted, though unwillingly, the fact that she could not live with her father as she had a completely different outlook on life. She wanted to live her life by her rules and girls in Surajpur didn't have that liberty. She'd come a long way, and couldn't go down that road again. If she'd learned anything at all since her mother got cancer, it was that all her instincts were backward. She had to plan out her moves carefully, charting the steps, distrusting her impulses, because her impulses always led her astray.

Sitting on the passenger side of his car, she took a minute to look around at the luxurious car. The door on the other side opened with a hiss, and Sanjay slid into the empty seat.

"I am not sure if I can wait any longer to have you," he said, an amused expression on his face.

Her eyes remained glued to his hands as he gripped the wheel. Strong, firm hands that had touched her with such tenderness. She swallowed a sudden wave of lust and stared out the window, watching the buildings disappear as he zoomed to her house.

He had been erect practically since they left the restaurant, and he had removed his jacket before the elevator stopped, had her apartment key at the ready and his arm firmly around her waist as the doors opened to the subtly lit hallway.

He propelled her towards a door at the end of the hallway, inserted the key hurriedly with force he'd use to insert himself into her moments from now, and then he flung open the door to the apartment. They stumbled, grabbing hold of the table to right themselves as the door closed shut behind them.

As her breasts brushed against his chest, the sheer material rubbed across her nipples and sent tingles of awareness shimmying up her spine. He was all hard muscles beneath her hands. Swallowing hard, she let her gaze stroll down his chest. He still wore pants, but she didn't miss the enormous bulge behind the zipper of those pants. He grinned and pinned her against the wall, his palms resting beside her shoulders, effectively trapping her in place. They stared at one another, neither moving. Trisha could hardly breathe with him this close to her. She could smell his musky scent, feel the heat of his flesh, and shivered.

His gaze dropped to her body as he gently pulled out her dress. She moved her hands upwards on cue, allowing the dress to leave her body and fall away. He unbuckled her bra, exposing her breasts to his gaze. He brushed the back of his fingers across her nipple, and she gasped at the shock wave that tiny contact sent inside her. He turned his hand, gently cupping her breast, weighing it before pushing upward and squeezing it within his palm.

"You have made me go crazy Trisha, but I hate it when you fight with me." He murmured, leaning closer, resting his elbow against the wall above her head. His free hand slid lower along her ribs to her hip. Trisha held her breath, unable to move. Not that she was willing to. He had a power over her she didn't understand, didn't want to understand perhaps.

"Right now, I am going to put up a fight with you, and I am sure you will like it. I know you like to force yourself upon me." She swallowed as his hand slid around and cupped her buttocks, squeezing it before sliding back up along her ribs. His hand moved lower, down her thigh, then back up again to swipe around her hip.

"Do you want me to kiss you yet?" he teased.

"No," she replied, continuing the game. But her body ironically said something else entirely as he cupped her buttock and pulled her hips from the wall. He pressed his thigh between her legs, putting mild but persistent pressure against her.

"No, I don't want you at all." She smirked.

"Liar," he said, his lips thinning out into a grin. "You are not putting up a real fight, Trisha." *I want you to put up a real fight. Then it would be really ecstatic to force you into lovemaking*, he thought. His palm squeezed her buttock hard, pulling it towards him and causing the sensitive area between her thighs to rub against his leg. The coarse fabric of his pants caused friction, sending heat blazing through her veins. She closed her eyes, fighting the desire to groan in pleasure. He slid his fingers inside her and she gasped.

"It's going to feel good when I get inside you," he murmured.

She shook her head. "No, you can't do that. I won't let you do that."

"I will get inside you, Trisha, even if you put up a fake fight. I know it, and so do you."

"No way! I don't think you are capable of doing that." She shook her head again, motivating him to force into her. He moved his hand around to the front and slid two fingers deep inside her, making her cry out as he thrust deep enough to push her to her toes.

"I like that," he whispered. "The sound of your moans. Such a randy sound."

She bit down on her lower lip, swallowing her own whimpers of delight as he slowly moved his fingers inside her.

"Your body can't fight with me, no matter how hard you try to hide it." His voice sounded coarse with desire, sexy, and it sent shivers running down her back. "You are mine and I would take you the way I want to, whenever I want to."

He pulled out his fingers. Her hands fell to her sides, fisting in the material of her panties as she forced them down to allow him all the freedom. He turned his hand so that the butt of his palm pushed against her, sending prickly lines of pleasure from there directly to her core. She groaned as the pressure inside her built from deep within. Her fingers fisted in the belt of his pants, holding firm as a thousand pinpoints of light exploded behind her eyes. She ground herself against his hand, riding out the waves of pure ecstasy.

"The night isn't over," he whispered, and she squeezed her eyes shut. "I haven't even kissed you yet."

He could feel her heat, smell her arousal, and his manhood threatened to rip open his pants. He was so damn hard.

"Sanjay…please," she whispered, her eyes demanding for him to understand.

He continued stroking her. "You're mine, Trisha," he whispered. "And you need to remember that." There was something deeply obsessive in his tone.

She swallowed and shook her head in denial. "No, I am a free bird." She was so wet he could hardly keep himself from taking her right now.

"Sooner or later," he whispered, brushing his lips over hers in teasing sweeps. "You'll give me the rest."

"No," she continued the denial game.

Her fingers dug into his sides as she frantically fought her desire. He always liked how she fought him; he enjoyed the chase, the denial and the forceful seduction.

He took off his shirt as her fingers moved to the buttons of his pants and jerked at them, liberating his manhood from the tight confines of his pants. Cautious fingers wrapped up his length, and he moaned. His teeth scraped along the sensitive flesh just below her ear, and she dropped her head back against the wall with a thump. She gave up all the fighting. What he was doing felt so damn excellent; she didn't want to fight anymore.

Squatting, he picked her up into his arms. She wrapped her arms around his neck, holding tight as he stood easily and carried her towards the bedroom. He laid her on the bed, leaned over her and cupped her cheek, turning her so she faced him.

"Trisha," he said, then sighed.

"I hate you. You always try to control my life," she said.

"I know," he replied. "But that doesn't change the fact that I want you…or that you want me."

She shook her head, swallowing down a lump in her throat.

"Just get it over with," she snapped.

He laughed, leaning down to kiss her brow. "I will absolutely not get over with it." He lay over her, his body covering hers from head to toe. "I plan on taking my time and making sure I enjoy every single second," his lips swiped across hers, his thighs spread hers, and his manhood pressed just inside her entrance. He thrust forward, burying only a tad inside her, and she gasped, lifting her legs to envelop his waist. Her vertical lips burned, stretched tight as he pushed in farther inside her. She held her breath, struggling to accommodate his thick manhood as he forced his way deeper before pulling back out. He pushed forward again. She could feel every inch of his thick heat throbbing inside her as he pushed deeper, filling her even more. She panted at the completeness, the burning pressure as he pulled back, then thrust forward again, this time going really deep.

She moaned, digging her nails into his hips. Sanjay groaned, grasping her hips with one hand to hold her still.

"You're so tight. I want to go faster on you. I hope that's not a problem?" he asked sarcastically.

She nodded, uncertain she could even speak at that instant.

"Answer me," he commanded, but in a soft and controlled tone.

"No, you can't go faster on me."

Her denial made him rock hard and he groaned as he ground deeper into her, sending shock waves of stinging sparks through her body. She allowed him to command her as she knew he couldn't do the same with his own wife. Maybe that was the reason he was so hooked on to her.

He rose above her onto his palms and amplified the rhythm of his thrusts. The position pushed him deeper, and she whimpered in pleasure, almost certain if he went any deeper he'd come out her throat. He thrust harder, scooting her along the bed as he pushed into her. She met every hammering thrust of his hips with one of her own, pushing back as he pushed into her. She was totally soaked inside, and she enjoyed every bit of it. She was so close, she could feel it just out of her reach, building higher and higher.

She closed her eyes, bracing against the onslaught of sensation travelling through her body. With a thunderous scream, she crested. Every part of her exploded outward in a mass of awesome sensation that almost took her breath.

"I want to come," Sanjay snarled and then thrust harder, pounding deeper than he had before. Trisha screamed again, combating against the desire to pass out as wave after wave raced through her. She convulsed around his manhood, as he shouted and found his own release. He dropped back down, covering her body with his, raining soft kisses along her neck.

"Look at me, Trisha," he commanded, and at first, she refused. He gripped her chin, forcing her to meet his hard stare. "I said look at me."

She narrowed her eyes, her mouth set in a hard, firm line. "I'm looking. What?"

He snickered, his lips twitching in sudden amusement. With a soft chuckle, he let go of her chin. "You're such an aggressive little thing," he said.

She stared up at him. "You can't even imagine what I am."

Bharti Kapoor was out shopping in the large Palladium Mall. An attractive woman in her thirties, her long shiny black hair was tied neatly with a Louis Vuitton clip. She was dressed in a beige pantsuit with an ivory silk shirt and beautiful gold jewellery. Her eyes reflected that they had once been more cheerful. But outwardly, she was slender, fair, well-dressed, and well-coiffed.

Just like a bee is attracted to honey, she was attracted to malls. Because shopping was the only thing she thought gave her momentary happiness in her hollow life. She walked in effortlessly as the glass door automatically opened to welcome her with open arms.

She saw many women, a whole lot of teenagers, fewer men, and no one dressed as impeccably as she was – in a perfect fitting Prada suit and high Jimmy Choo heels. Just as she took a few more steps, the aroma of perfumes hit her. She turned towards the Burberry store and walked in. So many perfumes to choose from! She tried a few until she found the right one for herself.

She then went to the apparels section. After going through what seemed like hundreds of outfits, she finally found something she thought might work for her. The pants were cut similar to jeans, but were made out of a lighter material. She lifted them and ran her hand across the soft, suede-like material. She grabbed two pairs and two tops, as well as shoes. Just as she made her way to the counter, a satin tunic caught her eye. It was gorgeous. On impulse, she decided to try it on and quickly headed to the dressing rooms.

Once inside, she studied herself in the three-way mirror. The tunic was perfect. The way it felt against her skin and clung to every curve of her body, even she couldn't resist staring at herself. With a naughty grin, she wondered what Sanjay would think if he saw it.

The lace hem rested about mid-thigh while the slit went all the way to her waist on both sides. Underwires pulled her breasts together, making it appear she had much more cleavage than she really did. It was definitely a tempting outfit. It was something she had never bought for herself. But somehow today she thought she wanted to buy something different that would help her to ignite the passion in their love-less marriage. She wondered if she would be able to tempt Sanjay with this outfit. Lately, Sanjay had not even been looking at her.

Once she had tried everything and was satisfied, she handed over her credit card at the counter, signed the slip, and watched as the showroom sales executive tenderly wrapped the expensive perfume in a purple wrapping paper tied neatly with a pink ribbon and placed it in a nice pink shopping bag. The other stuff was placed in the standard Burberry checkered shopping bags.

"I hope to see you again, Mrs. Kapoor," the saleswoman smiled as she handed all the bags to her.

"Thank you for the lovely service." Bharti returned her smile.

Bharti stepped outside and went on to the escalator. The second floor was much more silent and lined up with many premium designer brand outlets. She loved this floor, with its respectful and hushed atmosphere of uncompromising service. This was where the elegant wives would shop. This was where the salespeople knew you by income level, and even hand-picked outfits for you to choose from. The shops were so premium that some people got intimidated to even step in.

But not her. She confidently stepped inside her favourite Chanel store. This store had a clientele so wealthy and so in love with fashion, they could afford to have what was new and one of a kind for as long as it remained one of a kind. And when they got bored or saw someone wearing their hot find, they would come again and buy the latest collection.

She looked through the display case and pointed out her selection. Shopping was her favourite pastime as her husband Sanjay was never there for her. More so now; there had been long business trips and late night meetings, and he seemed to have become completely involved in his work, almost to the exclusion of all else. She had found herself alone, and eventually decided she couldn't bear to sit around the house all day, so had come to the mall.

Her perfume shopping had gone good. Add to that the necessary trendy haircut at Keune and buying those sexy outfits. And the orgasmic Jimmy Choo shoes. God, she loved shoes. As she finished her shopping and stepped out of the mall with shopping bags, she fell in the way of three guys running like maniacs. She had barely steadied herself when one of the boys collided with her with great force and she fell down. The guy quickly got up and ran again.

Helping hands around her got her to her feet. She discovered that her bag with the new shoes was missing, she had somehow or other cut her arm and her hair fell around her face.

"Are you all right?" Bharti spun around at the sound of the deep voice and stared at the gorgeous man before her. A dark-haired young man grabbed her arm and helped her on her feet. There was a short girl standing next to him. Bharti noticed that he was young and had a masculine face, with strong cheekbones and a cleft right in the middle of his chin.

There was something about the man's physical presence that took her breath away. A sort of overwhelming chivalry and vivacity that emitted a magical magnetism. He had the hard, rock-solid build of an athlete; there must not be an un-toned muscle in his body. His black hair was shining in the sunlight. His eyes were only pools of shadow and she could feel them sweeping her in a manner she had not yet learned to take for granted.

She was used to guys giving her a quick glance once-over, their eyes sweeping across her face and down her body in a blink. But she felt that he looked at her like nobody else had ever done before. Bharti tried without success to battle the unreal sensations that were turning her stomach to butterflies and her brain to butter.

Ankit looked at the cut on her arm. "Look," he said to Bharti, "if it's okay with you, then I would like to help you. Please come with me to a chemist shop or a doctor nearby so that we can get this bruise bandaged.

"Who are you? I don't believe I know you," she said in a voice more husky than usual, with a little catch to it.

"That makes us even." His strong mouth quirked into a smile that revealed white even teeth. "I don't know you either. But I plan to help you if you would let me."

There was a vibrant intimate quality to his voice that thrilled Bharti to the core. He seemed to be enormously self-assured and mature and his kindness brought a smile to her face. "Well…" started Bharti as she looked up at this guy. He was a gorgeous man, and most definitely way too sexy for his own good. He was dressed in street clothes, and the casual jeans and blue button-down shirt was suiting his frame.

The short girl pulled Ankit a bit away from Bharti and spoke in a hushed tone. "We need to go and meet my friend. You know how important it is for me. Let's go. I am sure the woman can take care of herself," said the short girl crossly.

"Why don't we do one thing? You go and meet up with her and I will join you as soon as I am over with this. The cut on her arm looks bad and I think I should help her," Ankit replied in a concerned tone.

She stomped her foot on the ground, unhappy with Ankit's decision and walked towards the mall. Ankit walked back to where Bharti was standing. He looked at Bharti and nodded, the genuine concern on his face making him appear boyish and all the more charming.

"I am sorry if it's a bother, but I just realised I won't be able to either drive to any clinic nearby or carry all these shopping bags and walk around looking for one on my own with blood oozing out of my arm at that pace. It's really nice of you to help me. Could you please take my precious shopping bags?" said Bharti with a slight smile appearing on her lips. She lifted up her shopping bags and handed them over to him and the two of them walked to find a doctor.

Ankit took hold of her arm and guided her through the mass of people.

"You can start by telling me your name, unless you plan to rob me off my shopping." Bharti tilted her chin in the slightly defiant attitude she always adopted when situations unnerved her.

"My name's Ankit Arora. What's yours?"

Bharti glanced at him. She guessed he must be about twenty-five years old. She found him uncomfortably attractive.

"Mrs. Kapoor," she said firmly.

He gave her a weird look. He was amused at her comment. "Mrs. Kapoor, really?"

The cut on her arm was hurting her but she was happy that there were still nice people who went out of their way to help others. Ankit spotted a chemist shop some distance away and led her in.

"We need some butadiene, antiseptic cream and some bandage," Ankit told the chemist across the counter. The chemist handed over the stuff to Ankit and he quickly paid him off.

"Come on," said Ankit to Bharti, "I'll fix your wound up." He took her onto the side counter. "So where's Mr. Kapoor right now? Do you want me to call him so he can come and pick you up?" he asked earnestly.

She looked at him composedly. "He's away for work."

"By the way, it will be nice if my patient told me her name. After all, I deserve that much, don't you think?" He smiled at her.

"Bharti Kapoor."

"That's a beautiful name, I must say. Wonder why you were hiding it behind the surname," he replied.

They looked at each other for a long moment before she looked apprehensively at the floor. This is bizarre, she thought. What am I doing here with this boy? What would Sanjay think? I must get out of here right away. This is not right.

Ankit skilfully cleaned her bruise with a cotton swab dipped in butadiene and then neatly tied a bandage over the cut on her arm.

"Thanks for all your help Ankit. You seem to be a really nice person. To be honest, I have met someone who believes in selflessly helping others after a long time. Never let this quality disappear."

"Sure."

"I must get back to my car now. It's really kind of you to have taken all this trouble. I have people expecting me at home, and they will be concerned if I'm too late."

"Sure, I understand," he said. "I'll carry your shopping bags to your car if that's ok with you, Bharti?"

"Y…Yes sure, why not!" She was mesmerized by his sweet and kind disposition.

Ankit fell into step beside her. "Did you enjoy your shopping?"

"Yes." Bharti turned her head in his direction, appreciating the fact that he was trying to strike a small conversation. The man had a comforting presence that made her feel safe and protected. "You know, you really don't have to keep me company. You can go back to your friends in the mall if you want."

"Actually you did me a favour."

"Really? I was thinking otherwise."

"No, actually I had no mood to step out of my house today but my friend literally pushed me to come here, and as you can see, I am not very good at saying no to people." He smiled sheepishly.

They walked in silence to where her car was parked. He helped her in. "I hope you don't mind my asking, but which part of Mumbai do you live in?" he enquired politely.

"Nariman Point."

"I guess we're neighbours! I live very close to that area." He stood on the road leaning against the car door. "Would it be too much to ask for a ride back to Nariman Point?"

"Are you sure you don't have to go back to your girlfriend?" She said anxiously. She just wanted to drive off from here and leave him standing there. She knew how attracted she was to him, and somehow she felt her inner self very exposed to this guy.

"Oh, she is not my girlfriend. What gave you that idea? She is just a friend. And if you agree to drop me, I would text her so that she doesn't get worried about me."

He looked incredible. Even more so than the last time she saw him a few seconds back, with his wide shoulder leaning against the door and his arms crossed in front of his chest. Bharti was touched by his warm gesture of helping her. She wanted to thank him and maybe by dropping him she would in a way help him back. But she was confused if she could start getting friendly with a complete stranger.

"Sure, come sit," she said tentatively.

His presence made her heart flutter wildly. Bharti was confused with her mixed emotions and tried to take a rational decision. What harm could a ride with a stranger do? He seemed to be a nice person, she thought. She turned the key and the car buzzed to life. Bharti drove towards Nariman Point, while Ankit sat silently beside her, his silence making her even more aware of his presence. Eventually she spoke. "Your girlfriend isn't going to be too pleased with you, saying you would be back and then just disappearing."

"Like I told you earlier, she is not my girlfriend, and I just texted her that I won't be coming back. Don't worry about her. I am sure she'll survive. But I am happy that you are so concerned about my love life." His lips curved into a naughty grin.

They lapsed into silence again. She decided that when they reached the destination, she would stop the car, just wait for him to get out and then bid goodbye and drive away quickly. She would give him no chance to talk about seeing her again or exchange numbers with her. Subconsciously, she knew he would want to do both.

"You are really different than others," he said.

"What does that mean?" she replied, startled.

"I mean you are quite different than the other people I hang out with. All my friends are really immature and shallow. But you are deep. Deep as an ocean, with secrets hidden in your heart."

"I am not able to understand what you are saying," she said defensively.

"I am sorry to be so blunt, but it seems that you are really lonely. You have been shopping alone in the mall and when you got hurt, you had no one to call. I actually feel that there is no one waiting for you at home."

Her first reaction was one of fury. She wanted to stop the car and tell this guy to get out. *But wait a moment! What he was saying was the reality of her life. Hear him out, what damage could it do? She was inquisitive too. How could a complete stranger know her so well?*

She forced a smile. "How can you be so sure?"

"I am sure because I remember the days when my girlfriend left me and I used to sit alone in my house for hours. You have the same look in your eyes. The only difference perhaps is that your husband hasn't literally left you."

"We've reached Nariman Point," she said quickly, and swerved the expensive car abruptly to the side. "Thanks for trying to sum up my personality and life in one sentence. But let me tell you that you hardly know me." She summoned up strength to put up a straight face at the handsome stranger. A stranger who could see through her hollow life.

"Maybe you are right. I am sorry I tried to judge you. I would like to know you more though."

She was stunned at his advance and turned to look at him. His eyes penetrated deep into her soul. She was worried that she was losing control. She mustered courage and said, "No, you can't know me more. I love my life and my husband. And I think we both should part our ways and go back to where we belong."

Ankit remained calm. Bharti felt that his smile could make time stop. She swallowed the lump in her throat.

"I would like to see you again, Bharti. I think you need someone like me. And more than that, I need someone exactly like you."

"No."

"Would you like to exchange numbers just in case you change your mind?"

She smiled, looking down at her lap. "Sorry. No. That would be a mistake."

"Would it help if I promised not to be?"

Startled, she looked directly at him. His eyes were earnest, and she wondered what sort of life he'd led that he could even say such a sweet thing. What would it be like to be so sure of yourself that you could promise not to be a mistake? She didn't know. Couldn't remember a time when she'd been so sure of herself.

"You can't promise me this."

"I can, but you need to trust me for that," he said without blinking.

"But I told you I am married."

"Look, let us do it this way. I will leave my number with you and then it's your call. I won't ever force you for anything." He lifted her iPhone from the dashboard and dialled his own number. "This is my number and I hope someday I get the opportunity to talk to you again." He smiled at her and to her surprise, a slight smile appeared on her face too. He opened the door and got out.

She watched him go. He's a kind guy but knows nothing about me, she lied to herself angrily. *He is so young, but at the same time, so mature. I would probably like to talk to him again.*

She jerked out of her chain of thoughts suddenly. *I would like to what?* She asked herself disbelievingly. She had never had an affair, was a virgin until her marriage, and now this thought was in her head. Sanjay is a wonderful person and a great husband, she thought, a wonderful lover. When did he even ask her how she was doing? Was she happy? When was the last time he made love to her? Maybe three months ago, and that was maybe an eleven minute quickie out of which she derived no particular pleasure.

Moreover, afterward, he would turn the other side and go straight off to sleep and snore, and she would lie awake looking at the dark ceiling wondering for a long time how it used to be in the initial months of their marriage.

She stared at the screen of her phone where Ankit's number was displayed. She selected the number and the menu displayed two options: SAVE and DELETE. Her thumb moved left to right, in confusion over the two buttons. She kept debating in her mind and finally saved his number. She started the car towards her house which was a few minutes away. When she reached the house, the stillness made her feel miserable. The house was empty. It was really disheartening. Ankit was right. There was no one expecting her at home.

Bharti switched on the television in the bedroom and noticed that it was nearly 8 p.m. Sanjay had said he would be home around 10 p.m., so there were good two hours to kill. She had no intention of watching television, but it was nice to have some voices around her in the large empty mansion. She decided to call her mother and chat for a while on the phone.

Her mother's voice was calm and contented, "Hello, Bharti."

"Hello, Ma. How's everything?"

"Oh, everything is as great as it should be. I was just lying on the couch and watching the new program *The Shastri Sisters*. It's nice! And how is Sanjay? Did you have a nice weekend together?"

"Yes, Ma. It was a nice weekend," replied Bharti remorsefully.

"All right, then. I'll speak to you later in the week. Bye." She wanted to tell her mother how she was feeling, but she didn't want to spoil her mother's evening. She seemed to be in a very happy mood.

Feeling slightly hungry, she went to the kitchen and looked at the food that the maid had kept in the refrigerator. On looking inside the refrigerator, her appetite suddenly died. She picked up the orange juice and gulped down a few sips. There seemed nothing else left to do except to go to bed and wait for Sanjay.

An idea formed in her head when she thought of the bed and Sanjay. She rushed to her shopping bags and pulled out the sexy tunic she had bought. Maybe it was the right time to wear it and tempt Sanjay into an intimate lovemaking session. She held it up against her. *Well, this is perfect for tonight. Wait till Sanjay sees me wearing this.*

She left the tunic on the bed and decided to take a shower. At that moment, her mobile beeped. There was a WhatsApp message on her screen from Ankit Arora.

"Hi."

She waited. She didn't know what to do.

"Hi Bharti. This is Ankit Arora"

Bharti still didn't reply.

"I am sorry I didn't mean to upset you. I just said what I really felt about you. I hope you will forgive me."

"There's nothing to forgive," she typed calmly. *"It certainly didn't bother me, either ways."* She pressed send and waited.

"Thank God for that. I was really concerned. You know, I am pretty straightforward. When I like people, I mean really like them, I always seem to come on too strong. I don't intend to, but it just happens that way."

"It's OK. But I need to go now. I don't think I want to chat any further."

"A friend of mine is having a party tonight and I thought you might like to come."

"I'm sorry, I can't," she typed back quickly.

"No problem. I thought I should at least try and ask you out.

Anyway, good night Bharti."
"Bye Ankit."
"Bye."

She kept looking at the screen but no messages came after that, though his status showed that he was online. She was happy that he had not bothered her by asking again and again. She kept looking at the screen and wondered why she was waiting for another message from him.

She was secretly pleased that Ankit had messaged. It made her feel sought-after and wanted, a feeling she couldn't recall having had for a long time.

Tonight things would be different. She would make Sanjay realize that everything could and should be as romantic as it was when they first met each other. After all, just because two people were married didn't mean that romance had to go by the board. I'm only thirty-five, she thought; that's still very young.

She lay her hands against the wood of the door, gently pushing it open. The coolness of the bathroom was refreshing. She stood shivering in the bathroom, staring at the steam rising from the hot tub. She peeled off her clothes and lit some candles, hoping that the soothing smell would touch her senses. She tossed in a few spoonfuls of the bubble bath mix kept at the foot of the bathtub and stirred the water with her fingertips. The water temperature was delicious. The aroma from the bath salt marinated the atmosphere with a stimulating fragrance. She slid down to wrap her body completely in the soft silkiness of the textured water. She grabbed the small bottle of bath gel off the counter and rubbed her breasts. She slipped down into the water till her shoulders and then sank down on the edge of the tub to wrap her body completely in the aromatic water. She sighed. On the outside, she might pretend to be just like everyone else, but on the inside, she knew she was different. She always followed the rules. She had been a good wife. She'd never been out of step. Until now. Thinking about another guy wasn't her approach. She could say and do all she wanted, but in her heart she believed that she could make this marriage work for both of them. She wanted to love the man she was married to, but she wasn't sure if Sanjay still loved her anymore. So where did that leave her? She soaped her hands with the lemon shower gel. The heady scent reminded her of her encounter with Ankit. She cupped her breasts, soaping them carefully with attention to each rounded curve and underside. Her nipples puckered beneath her palms. She released a soft sigh and leaned back against the tub. Her hand wandered across her flat belly, her hipbone, then lower to tease her. She was moist and ready. Joining with Ankit meant meaningless, casual sex. Her heart pounded, and she felt like a raw need for having sex after a long time. Her throat choked with emotion. Pressure built behind her eyes, despite her best efforts. She slid a questing finger inside her. Her eyelids closed, as she bit her lip.

"Ah!" she groaned. Her breast rose and fell, and the musky scent of the shower gel filled the air. But most disturbing was the flash of thought. She was thinking about Ankit. She was completely lost in her dreams, and that worried her more than anything else. She sank down so that the water covered her mouth. Bharti didn't know whether to laugh or cry. The bathroom air was still heavy with moisture, the mirror steamed up despite the fresh air from an open window. She walked out of the tub and studied her body in the bathroom mirror as she rubbed it clean with a towel. I could do with going on a diet, she mused. Her legs were shapely but a little bit heavy around the thighs; her waist was quite slim; and her breasts, large and full, were still firm.

She slipped into the tunic; it clung to her skin appreciatively and she was delighted with the effect. She applied light makeup and combed her hair. Then she turned off the television and put on some soothing music. A glass of red wine would be good, she thought. There was a bottle of Merlot in the bar, so she went and got it.

Two hours passed. The wine bottle was finished, the music had stopped. The sexy tunic was replaced with a night suit. She was drunk and the emptiness of the house seemed to depress her. *Where was Sanjay? He had said he would be here. If he was going to be late, he could have at least called or messaged me. Perhaps he got stuck in another business meeting or...*

She picked up her iPhone and called Sanjay, her well-manicured nails glistening on the screen. The phone rang. Sanjay spoke speedily, "Look, I'm held up in a business meeting here. I had to drive over from the city to ND studios in Karjat, and the video shoot is still on. I am not going to risk driving back tonight, as this area isn't safe at all. I'll leave early in the morning and be home by nine. I promise."

"But Sanjay, I have been waiting for you." She tried to keep her voice pleasant. "Why couldn't you send me a message or call me earlier? Why are you telling me this when I am calling you? "

"I can't talk now, I am in a meeting. Why can't you understand such a simple thing?"

Her anger suddenly snapped. "I don't care whether it is a simple thing or not. I don't care about your business meetings either. Have you ever thought about me? I've had a bloody miserable week, and tonight I've just sat around waiting for you, and you couldn't even bother to call or message me. At least if I'd known that you would be coming late I could have made some plans. You're so selfish and think only about yourself and your business. You have not done good to me as a husband. And the business in which you keep yourself busy, even there you are not doing any good. You are a loser and I don't deserve such a life."

His voice was cold and dispassionate. "Like I told you, I'm in the middle of a meeting. And I am doing all this for our better future. I'll give you the remaining explanations tomorrow. Bye."

She looked at the phone screen. For a moment she sat very still, trying to soak in what had just happened. He had hung up on her; he hadn't even bothered to wait for her to say bye. Tears burned her bloodshot eyes and she closed them, not before a tiny rivulet broke free, sliding hotly down her reddened face. *Why did she have to face all this when she had been a good wife? When had love vanished from their relationship?* With the back of her hand, she removed the damp tear tracks from her cheeks.

"What are you going to do about this?" Bharti asked the sad-faced woman in the mirror. The back of her hand pressed hard to her mouth to control the sob, she fell to her knees and cried, again, over a man who did not respect her or love her anymore.

Frustrated, tired and so achingly lonely, she opened her WhatsApp and typed.

"Hi Ankit."
Immediately she got a reply from him. *"Hello."*
"I've had too much to drink, and I think I need to get out of this house."
"That's great."
"Is the party still on?"
"Yes and I am waiting for you," Ankit replied.

Sanjay looked at Trisha sleeping next to her and then glanced at the room. He wondered how she could afford such a luxurious house in this expensive Mumbai city. All her furniture looked expensive and she had an enormous wardrobe of designer clothes. She wasn't a successful actress and hence he assumed that some other boyfriend of Trisha would have funded this place. The mere thought of another guy in her life annoyed him.

Trisha had told Sanjay that she had left home at eighteen, and moved to Mumbai two years ago, all set to be an actress. Now she was twenty, very beautiful and sparkled like a star. But still, she was just an unknown actress with an advertisement or two in her portfolio. He had known her only four weeks and in that time she was always available. There didn't appear to be any other man on the scene. She had accepted the fact that he was married to Bharti, and didn't nag about it as a lot of women might do. She never asked him for money. She knew that Sanjay was completely in debt, but as long as he was funding their rendezvous, she never fussed about it. He decided that he had to find out more about her life, her dreams and how she managed her finances in this city. He decided to bring the subject up and get some clarity. He wanted full control of her life.

"Trisha, there is something I want to talk to you about," he whispered as they lay on the bed the morning after a furious bout of coupling.

Trisha yawned and stretched. *Oh God. Not again, she thought.* She didn't like it when Sanjay became an obsessed lover. She was getting used to him, his looks, his body and his needs. She knew how to avoid his questions. She wound herself around him, whispering sweet luscious things in his ear. A certain part of his body stirred, showing signs of interest. She knew everything erotic to say to a man like Sanjay; every way to tug and twist his earlobe, his mouth, his tongue; how to hold him and cradle him even as she was his erotic plaything, so tempting that he couldn't hold himself back. Sanjay's mouth curved in amusement.

She moved lower between his legs and took his manhood in her mouth and pulled on it, hard. His body jolted with delight, and she took him – slow and soft, sliding, pulling, nibbling at him, trying to wake him up from the morning slumber. She closed her mouth tighter around him. It responded by growing bigger, filling her mouth, deep and hard, the way it would fill her up between her legs. Sucking him took all her energy; she pulled at him and licked him until she felt his body stiffen.

"So you had some questions Sanjay?" she teased him.

"Yes…no." He breathed hard.

"Why don't you tell me what you want?"

He took her face in his hands and kissed her. Even with hooker lips, she was more precious than anyone he'd ever known. He brushed his lips across hers. Once, twice. He tugged fiercely at her bottom lip.

"Ouch, that hurts Sanjay. Can't you be a little pleasant while making out? Why do you have to be so rough?"

He paid no attention to what she said. He stroked her face, her hair. She smelled so good, so warm in the glowing morning. She groaned and pressed in closer. His breaths came in quick bursts, and she could feel his awakening as he brushed against her. His urgency felt like a racing car, and she was already burning. Wordless, she pressed her open mouth against his and tugged at his lower lip. Sanjay immediately cupped her bottom and pulled her against him.

She knew exactly where to touch him, exactly how to kiss him. Sanjay was burning up. She took his mouth in a blazing, sexually claiming kiss that left him moaning.

"You've got to slow down," she muttered.

"No," he protested.

"Yes," she said. She guided him to the iPod player dock, hit the power button, and let the trance music fill the crackling air.

Pulling her closer against him, he took her mouth again and began to move. Her heart hammering, her body clamouring for more intimacy, she struggled for her breath. "What are you doing?"

"We're dancing," he said.

"We're naked."

"I know," he said.

His chest rubbed over her breasts, tightening her nipples. His thigh slid between hers. He rocked his hard manliness seductively where she was moist and swollen for him. Sanjay inhaled deeply and drew in her scent. He wanted to drown in all the sensations she evoked. Everything about her drew him, teased him. She was so mouth-wateringly close, yet not quite close enough. His heart hammered against his ribcage and he lifted her mouth to his. The brush of her tongue over his, combined with her rhythmic intimate movements was so erotic he could barely breathe.

"You feel so good," he told her, sliding his hands a little below her waist.

"Oh, Sanjay," she groaned. "I want you—" She broke off when he kissed her again.

"What do you want?" he asked her, bending his head to kiss her once more.

In answer, she climbed in his lap with her legs straddling him. His body struggled for control, aching to push inside her, right there. When she looked up at him, her eyes were a shade darker. "I want you to touch me. You have to touch me."

Slowly, he leaned closer, his arm brushing against her breast. The slight touch was a heady torment, and her breasts swelled, her nipples throbbing against his chest. He cradled her body with his own, grazing his lips over her neck. She rubbed against him and he locked his hands on her hips and pushed against her. His manhood was hard and insistent, and she licked her lips, her eyes drifting shut. Her legs were young and strong and she held him tight. This is what Sanjay loved about her. She sometimes did a role reversal and became in charge of the sex, just like him. Maybe they were similar in many ways. There was something incredible about her. All fresh and young. Each time she moved, he answered. Each time he moved, she moaned. His hand skimmed lower, flirting between her legs. Even Trisha really didn't care. All she wanted was a release from the insistent throbbing between her legs. She rocked against his hand, biting her lip in frustration.

His hand slid between her legs higher and higher. Her stomach pumped, waiting. One heartbeat, then two, then… One finger slid inside her, then two. His fingers pushed inside her further than she could have imagined, and she enveloped him fully. She shivered, cold, then hot.

His lips brushed against her ear. "You are so wet."

"Oh." She groaned and rocked against the solid, snooping pressure of his fingers, her body crazy with rippling pleasure. She could feel each finger individually as he bore into her, could feel his thumb braced on her outside, felt the lushness of her body and the start of the sharp, steep climb to orgasmic oblivion. She let herself go, let herself slide into a long, slow leap of molten pleasure.

"Mmm," she groaned, writhing away from his invasive fingers.

She wrapped her legs around his waist tightly, needing to feel him inside her. He lifted her and took one step forward, braced her against the wall; she locked her hands around his nape. And then he plunged inside her. Sanjay staggered for a second; he needed to find control, and do it his way, but all his control had disappeared in front of Trisha. She was riding him. She was in charge of the situation. Her hips ground against him, and he started to move. Thrusting inside her, deeper and harder.

His eyes held her gaze, unflinching. The way she looked at him, with need and something more, made anything possible. For now, nothing could touch them. She was his.

She wrapped her legs more tightly around his body and welcomed his violent pumping, welcomed his ferocious kisses, his explosive sex. She welcomed and wanted everything about him with the same ferocity with which he was taking her. He drove inside her, over and over, determined to please her. In this, there would be no one but him. Her head rolled to one side, her hair falling across his shoulder. She bit her lip, and still he moved. Over and over.

A moan of surrender broke her lips. She was close. Her nails were piercing into his neck, but there was no pain. Instead, he moved faster, harder. He felt her muscles clench around him, saw her eyes go blank, her lashes drift downward. She began to gasp and shiver, and he smiled with satisfaction. He thrust inside her one last time, as far as he could go. His body jerked, a charge of energy pulsing through him. Then his climax came, the undeniable pleasure, the undeniable truth that he couldn't stay away from her.

♦

After a few hours of lazing around in bed, Sanjay woke up. Trisha lay beside him, her long hair in a frenzy around her face, her makeup smudged and washed out. She looked very young.

"You're like a small baby," he said, "sometimes innocent and sometimes mischievous."

"I like that. There was this guy, and he said the same thing to me, 'You're like a baby—'"

Sanjay interrupted her. "Please don't say that. There will be no other guys in your life, only me. I love you from the bottom of my heart and want to get married to you." He was shocked with the words he had just blurted out.

"You know, it's so astonishing," she said, "how very simple it is for you to propose to me. Let's get married darling, but don't let my wife find out!"

The only reaction he had to her words was a slight tightening around the eyes. When he got to the place where most people stop and respect personal space, he took two more steps towards her and looked into her eyes. He was fuming with anger. Yes, he had not actually meant it. All he wanted to ensure was that Trisha had no other guy in her life. He wanted her to be his and only his sweet possession.

"I could try and get a divorce from Bharti," he lied. He was never going to marry Trisha; he had a trophy wife who suited him much.

Trisha felt a sudden and unaccustomed surge of annoyance. "Are you going to get a divorce? I mean, really? And then what will be left with you? You are already in debts and I am sure your wife would take away whatever else you have. What will you tell your wife? What will you tell the bankers whose loan you have to repay?" she replied coldly.

The barest expression of confusion flitted across his face, as though he could not comprehend why she would ask such questions. "I don't know. But you don't worry about the money. You don't understand these things. See, I don't have to pay the loan. The company has to pay the loan. And if the company goes bankrupt, the banks can't take a penny from me." His voice was rough, filled with deceit and rudeness as he turned to glare at her.

"And as far as our future is concerned, I have already told you what I have stashed. That is not known to either the banks or to my wife Bharti. I am not so foolish." Sanjay chuckled, not too pleasantly.

The world darkened at the edges of her vision. Trisha tried to take a deep breath, but it seemed like something heavy had settled on her chest. "Your opinion of others is so low. You are so over confident that—"

Sanjay interrupted her, giving her no chance to speak at all. "Remember one thing, Trisha, I have become really possessive about you and this has never happened before in my life. A lot of girls come and go in this advertising business. But you have made a place for yourself in my heart." He pulled her to him forcefully. "I really want you and I can look after you and give you a good life. I don't want you to waste your life struggling to become a star one day. I'll give you all the money you need. Let's go and sell some of the diamonds."

She stared up at him. "There's only one little problem."

"What?" asked Sanjay.

"I don't *want* to marry you. Not even if you were not married, and we could run away and do it right now. And I care a damn about your money because it comes with a lot of baggage." She wriggled away from him and got off the bed.

"But what's the problem, Trisha?" asked Sanjay barely able to conceal his dismay.

She stood looking at him and continued, "I want to be a free bird. No strings. I want to do whatever I want, whenever I want. I don't want to get married to you…or anyone else for that matter. It is a stupid custom and it means nothing to me. It's like a golden cage for me where I would lose my freedom. And yes, I love you too, for now, and maybe just for today. But tomorrow, I may be in love with someone else, who knows? That is me. I don't pretend to be someone I'm not, so why don't you try and do the same?"

She busied herself in the kitchen while Sanjay got busy thinking about what he had just proposed to Trisha. Actually he wasn't sure if he could leave his wife Bharti. It was good to have a trophy wife for having a good image in the social circle he had. She had ceased to attract him sexually shortly after they were married, maybe because he got bored of her or maybe because he had too many opportunities. Or both. He had compensated for the sexual vacuum in his marriage by different affairs throughout the years; and to Bharti, he had been more than generous materially. She was the perfect wife figure. No, he definitely didn't want to leave Bharti. But he realized that he felt no particular guilt about being unfaithful to her. If she was unfaithful to him, then he would not be able to handle it probably. But that was not possible at all. The very idea of Bharti being unfaithful was bizarre.

Trisha was lying on the couch. She was wearing short baby pink coloured hot pants and an off shoulder white top. She looked amazing. Her hair hung around her shoulders in a thick black mass that his fingers itched to slide through again. The desire that immediately began to swirl low in his trousers only made him glare all the harder.

He tried to shake his desire off his mind and concentrated on the topic he wanted to discuss.

"I want to talk to you seriously Trisha."

She narrowed her eyes.

"I've been really concerned about how you manage your finances. This house looks very expensive…you must be paying a heavy loan and I want to help you out. I mean, really, where do you get the money to pay for all these luxuries?"

She sat motionless. It seemed to be the silence before the storm. Her eyes glinted dangerously. However, she managed to keep her tone pleasant. "Well, baby," she said amiably, "I do not interfere in your life and I don't want you to interfere in mine. It's none of your business. Why is it so difficult for you to understand such a simple thing?"

"Trisha, I want to know," he said piercingly.

She snapped, "I am not asking you for any money and how I manage my life is completely my problem. You need to get this straight that I don't like being questioned." She started to shout on top of her voice. "Just leave me alone!" She had tears in her eyes now, and he was stunned that he had provoked such anger. "I am not answerable to you. I am not your wife. If you have so many questions, then let's just forget this. I can't handle all this crap from you."

"All right," he said grimly, "let's forget this. If that is what you want." He marched into the bedroom and dressed hurriedly.

When he came out she was still sitting on the couch pretending to be reading the *Cosmo* magazine, hiding her face behind the magazine. She continued reading and didn't look at him.

"Goodbye," he said, and left the apartment.

As he banged the entrance door and stepped out, he instantly regretted this move. He knew he would miss her, but if he agreed to her now, he would be accepting defeat, and that he wouldn't do for any bitch.

He looked at his wristwatch. It was 3 a.m. He couldn't go home as he had already informed Bharti that he would come in the morning. He decided to spend the rest of the time on the office couch.

There he was, tall and stylish, his eyes lighting up at the sight of her. Ankit looked younger than Bharti remembered him. He wore a black shirt and light blue denims. She went weak with anticipation. He had fine hands, a fit body, and a sensual mouth; the expression in his eyes veered from amused to appreciative at any given moment, and he always seemed to be relishing that moment.

She had decided to wear a beige dress after discarding several other outfits. They met at a pre-decided spot. Ankit helped her out of her car and said he would drive, as he knew the way and she still had an arm bandaged. She gave him half a smile and an abbreviated wave.

"I'm glad you changed your mind. What did it? My unbelievable charm or the alcohol you had?" He looked at her. She was an enigma, this woman. Bold and reticent, passionate and distant. Open and shut. Completely fascinating. She was an attractive woman, with smooth hair and an elegant manner of dress. Intelligent enough. But she was also insecure and frighteningly needy.

She loved how he had phrased it, so delicately that it made her breathless just thinking about everything to come that he had not said. "I don't know." All the wine she had drunk and the rush to get ready had finally made her tired. "Maybe I shouldn't have come. I don't know why I am here, really."

He looked at her. "I'm really happy that you're here. And I am sure that you won't be sorry you came. It's going to be a great night."

Ankit was driving them along the Marine Drive. She hadn't even known he knew how to drive a car. Though of course he did, and he drove it with cool self-assurance. That was Ankit – confident, competent, and crisp as a fresh apple.

She, on the other hand, was freaking out.

"It's going to be fine, Bharti. Relax." He dropped his hand to her thigh and squeezed it through the fabric of her dress, her very expensive beige raw-silk dress that would be terribly wrinkled by the time they reached the destination.

Screwing her eyes shut, she concentrated on Ankit's hand on her leg. It was warm, heavy, and alive, and her body responded with the heat his touch aroused. If he could keep one hand on her at all times, she might make it through tonight.

No such luck. He returned his hand to the wheel to change lanes, and she tried in vain to smooth out her wrinkled lap.

They drove a short way along the Marine Drive until Ankit pulled into a street on the left and parked near a lounge called 'Dance by the Bay' and they went in. This lounge was the largest she had ever seen in Mumbai. And she'd certainly seen her fair share. Sanjay's favourite pastime had been bar-hopping, and he always dragged her along for the ride.

On the main floor was a huge square island made of wood, right in the middle of the room. It had tall stools all around it, and there were at least thirty tables scattered around the floor. Behind the island was a wide staircase that led to the second level. It circled the room on all four sides with a beautifully decorated railing. It had tables as well as couches and chairs spread about in small conversation areas. But what caught her attention was the window. It was amazing. It ran the whole length of the wall in front of them and went from floor to ceiling and she could see the beautiful starlit sky.

The large hall was full with various people, guys, girls sitting and standing, and everyone steadily drinking. People on the dance floor were dancing to their own tune. Many couples were dancing and kissing, but no one was taking much notice of them. After all, that was one of the best things about Mumbai.

Ankit squeezed Bharti's arm. "Come on, let's grab a drink," he said, leading her up to the bar. "My friend is a manager at this lounge and he will make sure that we have a good time. At least that's what he has promised me."

She was failing a lot around this guy. It ought to have been worrisome, or at least embarrassing, but his words had liquefied her brain and she just followed him.

The bartender poured a very large scotch in a glass and a red merlot wine. They had a couple of drinks and started enjoying the music and tapping their feet on the wooden floor.

"Let us go and dance," he said, and put his arm around her waist. She could feel the hotness of his hand penetrate her dress through to her skin.

Reaching out, he held her hand and tugged her against him. She gasped, arching back slightly as his palm splayed at the small of her back, holding her close.

"Don't," she said, barely above a whisper.

He was close enough for her to smell him, the scrumptious blend of merlot wine, scotch and a man that did something a little crazy to her body, a sort of drums-thumping-in-her-veins thing that was hard to overlook. She kept her eyes fixed on his chest, which didn't really help because it was a very nice chest in a very nice shirt, and she knew exactly what it would feel like under her fingertips.

Time to look somewhere else, she told herself.

She raised her eyes to the hollow of his neck, and then to the clean-shaven pointed chin that was waiting to be touched by her fingers. *Look somewhere else.*

His mouth. *Bad choice.* Oh, the things he could do with that mouth. She wanted him to kiss her so bad she could hardly think. Hell, she wanted him to jump on her right here in the club.

He wasn't an infatuation. He was a dark temptation.

A couple bumped into Ankit and he pressed full-length against her for a moment – not altogether accidentally, she suspected. It wasn't for long, but it was long enough for her to learn that he was hard as a rock and ready to party.

He braced his arms on either side of her head. "Bharti, look at me."

He tipped her chin up with his other hand and brought his mouth to within mere inches of hers. She inhaled the scent of whisky and hot, musky male, and every part of her flared to life. Even her nipples, which were flattened against his chest.

"Why?" His lips brushed across her softly, barely touching hers. "What are you afraid of, Bharti?"

She swallowed. "I'm not afraid of anything or anyone."

Liar, she told herself. She was afraid of plenty of things. But most of all, she was afraid of what he made her feel, what he made her want to do to him and have him do to her.

"We shouldn't be…" she began, but he placed his finger over her lips, stopping her.

"Shhh! Can I not kiss you just once without you fighting me?"

As he dipped his head to kiss her, she backed away. Her heart hammered in her chest with a need she found harder and harder to ignore. If he kissed her, she'd be lost, she knew it.

Swallowing nervously, she stood stiff as a rod, waiting to see what he was going to do. Would he stop? What worried her most was the knowledge that deep down she really didn't want him to. It wouldn't take much to make her melt. He'd proven that already.

Like a true gentleman, he stepped back. "I won't force you into anything. But I want you to be sure what you really feel in your heart, Bharti. You need to ask yourself why you are here."

As if he had said the magical words that touched her heart. He stretched out his hands and Bharti hugged him tightly. In the comfort of his embrace, she felt safe. Even in the noisy lounge she could hear his heart beating next to hers. It was long since she had had such a good feeling. The feeling of not being alone. The feeling of having someone close to her.

All she could do was watch in anticipation as his mouth lowered to hers. With a compassion that took her breath away, he sipped at her lips until she opened them, her body melting into his. He tightened his arms as his tongue leisurely explored and teased.

He was calm and patient, his lips soft against hers. In his arms, she felt loved and protected. It was such a different feeling than what she had with her husband Sanjay these days. Ankit was everything Sanjay wasn't.

Ankit's mouth eagerly devoured hers. He couldn't get enough of her taste. He wanted to rip her clothes off and bury himself inside her hot little body until she accepted that she had feelings for him. The velvety feel of her tongue sliding along his drove him damn near insane. She closed her eyes as she felt the intimacy of his tongue penetrate her lips. His mouth was persistent and demanding. She felt she should push him away but didn't have the strength; and anyway, she didn't want to. It was a long time since she had been kissed like this. Bharti stilled, her mouth was immobile beneath his questing lips.

His arm snaked around the small of her back, pressing her body against his. Her heart raced, and she burned everywhere. Without thinking, her hands slowly moved up his arms, feeling the firm muscles beneath the fabric. His lips brushed across hers, and she sucked in a breath. It was so sexy the way he whispered against her mouth. The way his teeth nibbled at her bottom lip made her crazy.

"Kiss me, Bharti."

After only a second's hesitation, she did. Wrapping her arms around his neck, she kissed him with all the passion she could muster. Her tongue delved and teased just as his had, causing him to moan deep in his throat.

By the time he broke the kiss, they were both breathing deeply. "Damn," he said. "I don't know how to say it, but this is the best kiss of my life." He leaned forward to kiss her back.

No, no! Her mind screamed but her heart said something else.

He put everything he had into the kiss, moving his lips and tracing the seam of her mouth with his tongue. Still she remained motionless. She gulped inwardly as he rained kisses on the corner of her mouth, across her jaw. She kissed him back, and their mouths met in mutual enjoyment.

They stood still among the dancers, lost in their own little world. His tongue explored her mouth, and she felt a sudden urgent desire for him. He pressed her very close and then released her.

"I think I have had too much to drink. I think I'm going to have a really bad hangover tomorrow," she said.

"Let's just focus on what we have in our hands today." He put his arm around her again, and kissed her cheeks, while his hand came up and gently cupped the side of her face. His lips were soft and warm against her cheek, and her eyes closed, her face turning toward his. Her body came alive with desire and need. She knew she should pull away, but couldn't bring herself to do it. Closing her eyes, she parted her lips, and he slipped his tongue inside. She moaned as his tongue coaxed and teased hers.

God, he could kiss.

"Bharti." His hoarse whisper blew across her lips just before his mouth captured hers in a kiss, and drove her wild. She could feel guilt gripping her heart, but she still couldn't stop. It was as though some invisible force drew them together, and she was helpless.

She melted against him, returning his kiss with a passion that matched his own. His hand slid from her cheek to tangle in her hair and pull her closer. She moaned as his mouth hungrily devoured hers, making her head spin, making her want things she had no business wanting.

Her body was on fire, tense and pulsating with need.

His deep, husky voice teased her ear as he whispered something she didn't understand. The thought that this was wrong nudged at her brain, trying to gain entrance, but she pushed it aside, wanting only to feel, to forget. She knew he could make her forget.

Ankit dropped his forehead to hers. Fisting his fingers in her hair, he held her close. "God, I want you," he whispered.

His voice was rough, almost gravelly sounding, and Bharti loved it. She loved his touch, his voice, and how he could make her feel.

He leaned down and kissed the side of her neck, gently nibbling with his teeth, and she shivered from head to toe. She could hardly breathe and gasped when he sucked at the sensitive flesh just under her ear. She felt weak and her head spun, and when she shut her eyes, everything whirled round and round. She could feel Ankit touching her, his mouth on hers, but it all seemed like it was happening to someone else.

"Let's go," he said.

With a huff of exasperation, she dropped her arms and caught up to him at the door. He opened it, allowing her to step out first. The spring like breeze blew, and she turned her face into the wind, breathing in the fresh air.

It had been so long since she'd felt so good. It felt unbelievable, and she smiled, savouring the indulgence, just in case she never got another such night.

Ankit pulled her in and made her sit in the car. He walked to the other side and sat on the driver seat. They seemed to be driving for ages, but really it was no time at all. Then he was helping her out of the car, and they were climbing into a lift, and then they were in his apartment.

In her drunken state she was surprised that she had time to register the details of the living room – the small kitchen, the foyer that connected those rooms to the entrance to the bedroom – before he nudged her in. The room was dimly lit, the bed was queen-sized, covered in a black and white checkered bed sheet with white pillows.

"Don't you think we have had enough fun for one night? Bharti asked.

His gaze turned dark, hot, making her breath catch. "We haven't even scratched the surface of things I want to do to you."

"Is that so? What things do you want to do to me?"

His palms slid lower caressing her hips. He watched her closely, his face still so very close to hers. She flattened her hands against his chest, slowly sliding them up, enjoying the feel of his thick, hard muscles as they twitched beneath her touch.

"Do you trust me?" he whispered, gently brushing his lips across hers.

She looked into his eyes and wondered if she could really trust him. There was something about him that made her think she could, but she couldn't get past the fact that he was a stranger. She'd made the mistake of trusting her heart with Sanjay. She couldn't do it again. The price was too high. When she looked back at him, he smiled seductively and a whole lot more than her arm began to quiver. She couldn't tear her eyes away from him as he took a step closer.

"Uh-huh," she whispered, barely able to speak past the lump of desire in her throat.

"Good." Bending, he picked her up in his arms. She squealed in surprise, wrapping her arms around his neck and burying her face against the warm flesh there. With a giggle, she kissed him just under the ear. He growled something in response, making her smile.

"I hope you meant what you said," he murmured, before tossing her onto the bed. "You're in for a hell of a night."

He shrugged his shoulders, allowing his shirt to slide down his arms and drop to the floor. Staring at his chest, she took in a deep breath to stabilize her pounding heart. Her flesh burned and her bottom lips clenched, both in lust and a slight hint of nervousness.

"What is it that you have in mind?" she asked, then squealed with laughter as Ankit grabbed her ankles and tugged her to the foot of the bed.

He didn't say anything, just softly kissed the inside of her knee, his palm slowly sliding the hem of her dress farther up her thigh. His eyes met hers, burning a trail directly to her insides, and she drew in a soft breath, waiting, anticipating what he had in mind. His kisses moved upward, barely brushing across her tingling flesh as he made his way to her panties. Putting his hands under her hips, he lifted them, then tugged them down her legs, tossing them to the floor. With a smirk that sent shivers down her spine, he gripped her hand, tugging her to her feet. She couldn't take her eyes off him as he bunched the fabric of the dress in his fingers, pulling it up her body and over her head. She didn't struggle, because, after all, this wasn't really happening.

His hands replaced the fabric, warming her flesh as his fingers explored her skin with agonizing patience. He placed feather light kisses along her shoulder, then her neck, making her knees weak. Just as they were about to buckle, he wrapped one arm around the small of her back, holding her upright. His teeth sank gently into the sensitive flesh on her nape, and she reached out to grip his upper arms. A soft gasp escaped her chest, and her fingers sank into his muscles. She was desperate to hold on, for if she didn't, she'd surely crumple in a heap on the floor.

Relaxing her fingers, she slid her palms up his arms and across his wide shoulders. Lifting his head, he brushed his lips across hers. Barely touching, his mouth teased hers until she buried her hands in his hair, pulling him closer. Her lips parted, allowing the assault of his sweet tongue to explore, tempt and tease.

"On your stomach," he whispered against her lips, and she nodded, moving to climb across the bed and lie on her stomach.

She felt the bed sink as Ankit climbed on, his thighs straddling hers. He leaned forward, his palms resting on either side of her shoulders. His lips blazed a trail down her spine, making her tremble in pleasure. Lower still, he kept going, his teeth gently nipping where the rise of her hips began. He kissed her slowly. The bed was soft, and she felt very comfortable. His arms were strong and warm, and his hands created a fantastic excitement in her. She felt him undoing her bra. But she didn't put up a fight as this was not really happening. It was a sweet dream.

"I'm not here," she whispered. "I'm in some other world." She wanted him to take her where no one else had. She wanted him to have that part of her.

He began to kiss her back, and then she was suddenly lost in a raging passion which seemed to go on forever and ever. She turned over to face him. The vulnerability in her eyes kicked out the cornerstone of his restraint and he did what he'd been wanting to do. He took her mouth, and a little taste only made him want more. He rolled his tongue over hers. She moulded herself to him as if she couldn't get close enough. She kissed him as if she wanted to consume and be consumed. The restless edgy need for her that he'd buried inside himself threatened to explode. He slid his hands over her bottom, curling her into his hardness, and she instinctively meshed with him, moving sinuously.

In her mouth, he tasted her resistance, the barest hint of unwillingness and wild voluptuous desire. Filled with an over whelming urge to possess her, he wanted to make the hesitation disappear. He wanted to be inside her.

He slipped his hands to touch her thighs and rubbed his mouth over the softness of her throat.

"Ankit—" she whispered in a breathless voice of both hesitation and invitation.

He felt the rapid thumping of her pulse against his cheek as he slid the loose bra lower and lower until one full breast was bared. He stared at her, aroused by the sight of her erect, dusky-rose nipple.

As he lowered his head, he could feel her holding her breath, waiting for him. He took her nipple into his mouth and she moaned. Her fingers slid beneath his hair, urging him on. The sensation of her in his mouth made him go wild. Sliding his hand lower, he sought her feminine secrets. Inside he found her wet and warm for him. He stroked the swollen bead of her pleasure until she began to pant.

"Ankit," she said. "This is crazy."

"It definitely is. Do you want me to stop?" he asked, caressing the tender spot.

She gasped and closed her eyes. "No."

"I need you to be with me, Bharti," he said, and plunged his finger inside her.

She clenched and clung to him, shivering. "I...I need to be with you," she breathed, her eyes dark with desire.

"I want to be inside you as deep as I can get."

She wanted the same thing. He could see it on her face. Holding his gaze, she lowered her hands to his hard, aching masculinity. Sliding his zipper down, she cupped and stroked him.

It was an exquisitely sensual sight. Bharti's gaze travelled to his bare manhood. She rubbed her thumb back and forth in increments over the tip of him.

Bharti sucked, drawing on his neck. His hands gripped her shoulders tighter, drawing her close and allowing her free rein. Bharti drew on the same spot for as long as it took to mark him. The idea of her mark on his neck, a hickey, thrilled her. It smacked of possession but that's exactly how she felt.

Bharti wriggled closer to kiss his mouth. Her mouth met warm, receptive lips. Masculine fingers threaded through her hair and hands cradled her head. Bharti moaned softly, writhing against him in silent demand.

He waited to feel like he wanted her less. He waited, but he still wanted her. "I have to have you. I have to make love to you tonight." He gazed into her eyes. She looked as needy as he felt.

"Do you want me?" he asked her.

"Yes," she whispered.

Bharti felt a sliver of sensual apprehension. He skimmed his hand possessively down her hip to her thigh. He kissed her and caressed her with a passion that never abated. He left no part of her body untouched. As if his fingers made love to her skin.

"Bharti." Her name came out as a low moan, coated with passion and possibilities.

Bharti didn't want to object anymore and she parted her legs almost immediately as he ran his finger at her sensitive area. The sensation rocked Bharti and fuelled her desire. His words thrilled her heart. And she wanted him just as fiercely as he wanted her.

She couldn't hold back a moan as his manhood slid between her thighs and claimed her. She held her breath, waiting, desiring Ankit's next thrust with every fibre of her being. He started with a lazy pace, as if they had all the time in the world. His fingers cupped her breasts, stroked her nipples, keeping up his slow, easy thrust and retreat.

Bharti strained against him, savouring the slap of his skin against her body. Her body pulsed and burned. Intimate kisses sent her spiralling and crashing. He held her tightly when she cried out. He brought her a pleasure she'd never known. It was his tenderness, however, that scored her heart. His gaze intent, he thrust inside her, and she gasped.

Ankit began to slide in and out of her in a rhythm that threatened to take her mind. The edges of the room blurred and there was only him above her and inside her. Only him. Again and again, he buried himself deeply inside her. With each stroke, she felt more taken. With each thrust, she felt her heart begin to slip. With each little sensual movement of her body, he grew harder and needier. She slid her fingers through his hair and cried out in pleasure.

His eyes held her crystal gaze, unwavering. The way she looked at him, with need and something more, made everything possible.

Ankit nuzzled behind her ear and nipped the soft skin there. He rocked against her, and deep inside her, she felt his manhood. Her body jumped in response, and Bharti tumbled into an orgasm that shook her clear to her toes. She lay there, savouring the aftershocks of her orgasm.

"Up on your knees, sweetheart; it's not yet over!" he whispered, and she turned around and rose up, her heart racing wildly.

He slid inside her again, making her gasp. She gulped at the blazing sensation, the pain as his manhood stretched her wider as it slid deeper.

"It's so good to be inside you," Ankit whispered, sending goose bumps along her flesh.

Rapture burned in her belly, making her wilder with unanswered need. She wanted him more.

"Aah," she moaned as he slowly moved in and out.

He pressed in deep. She gasped, pressing her hips back, spreading her thighs wider to allow him better access. With a scream, she dropped her forehead to the mattress, trying her best to remember how to breathe. She felt so full, so consumed; she never wanted it to end.

With a deep growl of his own, he pressed deeper still, then pulled out, only to plunder her again. Over and over, he thrust into her, sending her spiralling to the stars and back, only to do it again and again. She cried out her pleasure, screaming at him to take her deeper. He gave her all that she begged for, until she couldn't take anything else. With a shout, she fell into her final orgasm, her body shaking from head to toe, her mind a jumbled mass of nothing. He thrust once, twice more, before following her off that cliff, losing himself to his own release.

The silence in the room might as well have been as deafening as the rumble progressing inside her. Bharti began to shiver. She clung to him, wanting to hold on to the moment as long as possible. Ankit lifted his face from the hollow of her shoulder and placed a kiss on her head, inhaling the ornate scent of her hair. She shifted and stared up at him thoughtfully, her eyes full of doubts and questions. He smiled lovingly at her and touched her cheek with the backs of his fingers.

"I love you," someone said.

It all seemed like a dream. But it felt great to be wanted.

♦

Too bright. It was way too bright. Bharti buried her face in the pillow with a groan, trying to shut out the morning light. She must have forgotten to close the curtains last night. Head hammering, she reached for the bottle of water she always kept on her bedside table, but her fingers scrabbled through empty space.

No water.

A further waving of her hand produced no bedside table. Huh.

With a groan, she cracked her eyes open and turned her face just far enough to bring the wooden corner post of a headboard into focus. A very different hardwood headboard than what she saw last morning.

Not hers. Shit.

She rolled over and surveyed the room, which was more like a white cube with meagre furniture – just the bed, a tiny wardrobe, and a recliner facing a TV placed on a small glass table. Whoever lived here had taste. But no money.

She sat up, wincing as she waited for the hangover judge to pass his sentence. Headache: yes. Nausea: yes. Acidic stomach: yes. But none unbearable.

She ran a hand through her hair, and the soft cotton of a man's oversized t-shirt brushed her cheek. Drawing the t-shirt away from her neck, she peeked inside. She didn't have her bra and panties on. Shit.

Reluctant to subject herself to what a huge mistake she had done, Bharti sank back into the pillows and squeezed her eyes shut, making a courteous request to the universe to remove her from this situation and put her somewhere else.

Anywhere else. Home would be nice.

Damn it, she didn't want to be here.

Yet here she was. The question was, how?

A memory from the night before offered itself up: her hand wrapped around a wine glass, and the pinched voice of Ankit saying, "Cheers."

Oh, God! Ankit.

That glass of wine had turned into two glasses and then into three because her husband Sanjay had again not turned up home at night, leaving her sad, frustrated and lonely.

That had been her limit for the evening, established in advance. Three glasses of wine. But three glasses of wine wouldn't have impaired her memory or landed her in this bed. So what? She smacked her palm into her forehead. Maybe she had had the full bottle. And then more drinks at the party. She remembered finishing the bottle of wine and then meeting Ankit at the party. She remembered the dance, the drinks, the kiss…

Bharti turned her face into the pillow, which smelled of summer and clean cotton. She wondered how many different varieties of stupid one woman could be. A great many apparently, because she was here. Wherever here was. God, she had gone home with Ankit, had she? She'd been too drunk to remember any of it.

She pulled the comforter up over her face and willed her pickled brain to release the details of what had happened after the party. Her brain gave her snapshots of the echoing clomp of her heels to her car. The drive back to Ankit's house. Then, his hand at the small of her back, guiding her to the door. His keys in the lock of the flat.

She lifted the comforter up and checked. Yes, there he was. Ankit. Sound asleep. Right next to her.

She pushed back the comforter carefully and slowly swung her legs over the edge of the mattress, scanning the floor for the clothes she'd worn last night. No luck, but the sight of the floor brought back a sudden image of herself sitting splay-legged on it, grinning helplessly, arms tangled up in his. She could still feel his hands at her rib cage, large and warm, pulling her to her feet. Unzipping her dress.

Bharti took a deep breath and let it out slowly. It was time to find a bathroom, locate her clothes and get the hell out of Ankit's flat. Ankit's life.

The bedroom door opened onto the hallway of a modest flat. The main entry was at one end, and that had to be the kitchen at the other. Which left one closed door on her left and one door directly across the hall from the bedroom. Bharti crossed her fingers hoping it to be the bathroom. It was.

She splashed some cold water on her face, working up the nerve to look in the mirror. Oh God! After scrubbing her makeup as best she could with cold water, she ran moist fingers through her chin-length, wispy black hair in a pointless attempt to restore some semblance of a style.

She rinsed out her mouth with water, beginning to feel almost human. She searched for a hand towel to wipe her face, but she found Ankit's work trousers hanging on the door. An identity card was hanging from the loop in the trousers – Ankit Arora, Sales Manager, Ethos Jewellers. She sighed. At least she knew who she was sleeping with and that he had not lied to her.

The shower felt divine, the water nearly hot enough to burn the skin, just how she liked it. She stayed under the shower for a long time, wishing she could wash the shame away along with the grime. Smoothing Ankit's spicy, man-smelling soap over her lower back and one side of her stomach, she remembered her rendezvous with Ankit last night.

This thing, whatever it was, this slip-up that had landed her in Ankit's shower had to be erased from her life. This was not her. She had never ever slipped up in her entire life. Then why now? Had Sanjay's absence created a vacuum in her life? Did she feel lonely every night alone in her bed? Or was it more than that?

She had to forget this had ever happened.

After drying off somehow with the t-shirt she was wearing, Bharti pulled on her panties and stepped out of the bathroom. Mostly headache-free and heading towards hungry, she ventured out. She quietly tip-toed back into the bedroom and searched for her clothes. When she found them, she dressed hurriedly. She again looked at Ankit to check if he was still asleep. He slept deeply. She stared at him for a long time, trying to capture him in her eyes.

She snagged her purse, wrenched the door open, and escaped, refusing to look back.

As she made her way to the street, she reminded herself it was probably for the best. She and Ankit didn't make sense together. After all, she was married to Sanjay.

She realized her eyes were watering and her chest felt sort of squeezed and squashed. But tears and moderate physical discomfort were no big deal. Symptoms like this were bound to strike on a day like today, when she was already off-balance from the whole waking-up-in-a-stranger's-house thing. And if the thought of never kissing him again made the squeezing sensation in her chest worse and the tears spill over, well, that's what she deserved for getting herself into this mess to begin with.

After a long sustained marriage, she'd let her guard down and had royally screwed everything up. But hey, the good thing about living in a big city like Mumbai was you could start over as many times as you wanted. She didn't have to see Ankit again. But how would she see herself in the mirror?

It was early morning and the streets were silent and empty. She sat in her car and turned on the ignition. Just like her, even her car was eager to go back home. Once there, she unlocked her house. Sanjay had not yet returned. She let herself silently into the house and went straight to her bedroom. Everything looked spotless and fresh.

Bharti stepped up into the bathroom and looked at herself in the mirror and cringed. Even with all these clothes on, she'd never felt more naked. She looked at herself wondering if she had done the right thing. Did Sanjay's frequent absence give her a right to be disloyal to him? She held her breath, waiting, examining herself. God, what the hell was the matter with her?

She cupped her cheeks and gave her a shake as she spoke. "Did I do this to make a point? Or did I actually want to do it?

Rubbing her hand down her face, Bharti let out a deep sigh. She didn't need this right now. She tried to bring herself out of the haze she'd been in for the last several minutes. She had stood there staring in the mirror, replaying in her mind the events of the night.

Lowering herself to the mattress, she covered up with the blanket folded at the foot of the bed. Sleep didn't come right away. Her mind kept racing, thinking about Ankit, the party at the lounge, and her rendezvous at Ankit's house. She closed her eyes and tried to think of something else. She would probably never see him again, she thought. Moreover, she felt tremendously guilty and angry at herself for having allowed it to happen. Yes, she had been drunk, but was that the real excuse? She had never imagined herself in the role of the unfaithful wife and it was not something she accepted easily.

She thought about Sanjay. In an hour or two she would have to face him, and that wasn't going to be easy. Eventually, exhaustion took over, her eyes closed on a tired sigh and she fell asleep.

Sanjay woke up a bit late. He looked around and realized that he was on his office couch. He went to the rest room. He came to himself standing in the restroom, staring blankly at the mirror. For heaven's sake, what had this girl done to him? Shaking his head in an attempt to clear it, Sanjay splashed water on his face, combed his hair, tucked in his shirt and wore his blazer.

It was 10.30 a.m., the perfect time to go back home. He sat in his car and zoomed out of the office parking. A few minutes later, he parked his car and opened the entrance door of the house with his set of keys. He walked across the living room and entered the bedroom. Bharti was asleep, curled up and buried beneath the sheets. He drew the curtains, throwing dazzling daylight into the room. She didn't stir. He paced the floor, coughed loudly, and when she still didn't appear to show any signs of waking, he finally went over and shook her out of her sleep.

Just at that moment, the telephone rang. Bharti suddenly felt very worried. What if it was Ankit calling to check if she had reached home? She wondered if she should answer it or should she let Sanjay pick it up, and then maybe Ankit would hang up immediately listening to his voice. She suddenly realized that her guilt was giving birth to these stupid thoughts. Ankit didn't have her land line number. *Phew!*

Sanjay swooped down on the cordless phone and spoke into the receiver, "Yes?"

He launched into a long conversation with someone from his office. She took advantage of his preoccupation on the phone and dressed up a bit to hide her guilt.

She wanted to ask him about his last night's meeting but she was worried that he would ask about her night and she was not sure if she could lie. Actually she had never lied to him.

"Do you want some breakfast?" Her voice squeaked with nervousness.

"No, I have to make some last minute arrangements. There's this party tonight to launch the Lasense lingerie television campaign.

Another party! She groaned inwardly at the thought of another party.

"I had forgotten all about it. You can meet me at the office at eight, and we'll go together from there," he commanded.

While Bharti prepared herself for yet another party, Sanjay lost himself in his own thoughts.

He felt happy about the party and smiled as he knew Trisha would definitely be at the party. She was the model being paid to be there at the launch. Plus, it was her big chance to meet the biggies of the business and she would never miss such an opportunity. He was already regretting the fight he had with her last night. He wondered if it would be possible for him to effect a quiet settlement without everyone in the party noticing them. He was also a bit worried that Bharti had become too suspicious and seemed to be asking too many questions about his whereabouts and not accepting his absence. Maybe she was beginning to suspect him, although this seemed unlikely, as he had managed to get away with various affairs throughout the years and she had never found him out yet.

He jerked off the thoughts and looked at his watch. His face lit up. In a few hours, he would be able to see Trisha again and resolve their fight.

♦

In the evening, Bharti dressed up for the party half-heartedly. She was in no mood to attend another party after her last night's adventure. Glancing down at herself, she adjusted her jet black jacket. The pants were loose at the waist but tapered at the bottom. The jacket opened down the front with no buttons and hung almost to her knees, with sleeves that were narrow at the wrists. It covered her from head to toe – not too dazzling, but that is how she wanted it to be.

Over the last couple of hours, she couldn't seem to get Ankit out of her mind. She thought that maybe if she saw him again she could figure out what it was about him that had her so involved. But Ankit hadn't called her or messaged her till now. She was not sure if she wanted him to connect to her or not. But maybe she wanted him to, otherwise, what had it all been? A quickie? A quick meaningless one-night stand? A few hours in bed with a handsome stranger?

She didn't think she'd gotten more than two hours sleep last night. She couldn't keep her hands off him, and the way he responded to her only made her all the more hungry for him the next time. She couldn't get enough, and that was not a good thing. *Next time? Was she already planning the next meeting?*

She left the house in a bad mood. She wanted Ankit to call or message so that she could tell him that she couldn't perhaps see him again, that it had all been a big blunder. She sighed. At least that way she would be able to reclaim a little self-respect by denying herself the pleasure of something she actually wanted. It was all so unanticipated. She had really never thought of herself as the sort of woman who could have an extra marital affair.

She had to stop thinking about him and the past night. She'd lost count of just how many times he'd made her come. And every time, he'd done it with such tenderness and care. She had to continually remind herself that it didn't matter. It was still wrong on her part to be involved with another man and she wondered how it had happened. She searched her mind and thought that it was perhaps because Sanjay had started ignoring her, or because he wasn't there for most nights or because her sex life was in ruins. But then, just as a good wife would conclude, she finally concluded that it must be her fault only.

She decided to try and erase the previous night out of her life and to work hard to make things better between herself and Sanjay.

♦

Trisha came very late to the Lasense party. She was supposed to come earlier to interact with the client, but she chose not to. After all, she was a free bird and did what she felt like. Sanjay had been waiting for her, and suddenly spotted her. She came and stood next to him, looking gorgeous, and whispered, "Hello, Mr. Kapoor. How is the launch going?"

Sanjay became very uncomfortable in her presence. His guilt reflected on his face. He was standing talking to a group which included his wife and many press journalists. Trisha noticed them and smiled slightly. People were looking at Sanjay in anticipation, waiting to be introduced to the hot girl who had just entered the group. At last he said, "Oh, this is Trisha Mehra, the model for our television commercial. She is here for the live presentation of the product to the press."

Trisha smiled at the group. She was blushing and her eyes looked droopy. Sanjay knew at once that she was a little high on alcohol. She wore an extremely low cut red dress, her hair was piled neatly on her head in a tight knot and a few tendrils brushed her cheek .The red sleeveless dress hugged her body, complementing her curvy figure.

The women in the group found themselves standing up straighter and throwing out their bosoms, as if in response to this unexpected challenge. The men were all noticeably impressed.

"Trisha Mehra?" A small reporter with eyes gleaming with malice stepped forward. "I want to know what do you really think of the products you advertise, the Lasense lingerie?" His eyes shot towards her cleavage.

Trisha understood his intentions, but played along. She knew he was a reporter and could possibly give her the publicity she was looking for. She flapped her extended eyelashes and gave him one of her hot, sexy looks. "Actually," she said at last, "I think the lingerie is really good. I believe in endorsing only those products which I am sure are good for the consumers," she lied. "But I have some more interesting gossip for you. I am sure you would be more interested in listening to something that's newsworthy."

The reporter nodded with excitement.

"I've got someone with me who is going to cast me for his next big movie." She waved her hand and called out. "Abhinav, Abhinav! Why don't you come here? Someone wants to meet you eagerly."

Sanjay flared. He hated Abhinav and knew that Trisha was doing all this to make him jealous.

Abhinav walked over to them. And then he was looming over them, impeccable in a Burberry suit, Armani shirt, Burberry tie, and Hublot watch. It wasn't as if the crowd was just impressed by the labels, it was him. The entire package – his height, his elegance, his utter comfort in his skin. He wasn't handsome in the classical sense, but he knew who he was and commanded attention; he had unmatched confidence, impeccable manners, and cool grace, though with subtle shades of arrogance.

He started speaking about his new movie and the journalists left Sanjay and gathered around him. Sanjay felt like a fool standing there and hated the fact that the show had actually been stolen from him. It was his day. He was supposed to be the big celebrity. But Trisha had ruined it for him by bringing in Abhinav to the party.

Trisha shot Sanjay a triumphant look.

The reporter was most interested in Abhinav Deo. He knew it was difficult to get his time. "Sounds great, Abhinav. Perhaps we could do a piece about you on page 3, or your young actress." He shot a glance at Trisha.

Before Abhinav could respond, Trisha jumped in. "Yes, that would be great." She smiled. "I'll give you my phone number."

Sanjay could not stand it anymore. He gripped her by the arm, smiled tightly, and said, "I hope you will excuse us. Trisha is here for a specific reason. She needs to get ready to demonstrate the products to the journalists. I think she's due to start the launch pretty soon, so I better get her over to Manoj Bhatt."

"Oh, well, Trisha," said the reporter, "Thanks for your number. I will call you and we will see how we can help each other. He looked at her luscious legs and then her breasts, as if capturing it in his memory for later use. He turned over to Abhinav and joined the discussion on his movie.

She gave one last radiant smile to Abhinav and followed Sanjay.

As soon as they were a bit away, Sanjay burst out. "You're really drunk. Where have you been all evening? You were supposed to be here by 7 p.m. And why have you got Abhinav with you? What are you trying to prove?"

She gave him an unruffled look. "Sanjay, baby, you are nobody in my life, so why don't you just leave me alone so that I can make my future. And I had an invite for two people. So I got my date with me. Plus, I think it has added a zing to your boring launch party as most people are interested in meeting Abhinav."

"Don't act smart with me," he said in a low voice. His grip tightened on her arm.

"I'm going to create a scene if you don't let go of me," she said softly. "I'm tired of you bossing me around. Like I told you earlier, I'm not your wife who has to answer questions and give a detailed account of every second of my life."

At that moment, Manoj Bhatt rushed up to them. He saw Sanjay forcing in on Trisha and wondered what was happening. He thought of asking Sanjay but didn't dare, as Sanjay would instead find faults in the launch and shout at him. So before Sanjay could shout on him, Manoj put up a marvellous act of shouting at Trisha. "What is going on?" he asked. "Trisha, you were supposed to be here two hours ago. We're waiting to unveil the display. Please get ready quickly. We don't want to be here all night!" He tried to steer away from Sanjay's stern look and then looked at Trisha and took her by the arm to the green room.

Abhinav Deo sidled up to Sanjay while Bharti was busy talking to a few other guests across the other side of the hall. "Your Trisha Mehra is quite a good catch," he said with a smirk. "I bet you have casted her in the bedroom by now."

Sanjay glared at him.

"What's that look for?"

"What look?" Sanjay growled.

"The 'don't-touch-her-at all-she-is-only-mine' look."

He turned away and brought the glass to his lips, taking a sip. "I don't know what you're talking about." Sanjay snorted.

"I may have misjudged your look, but I certainly haven't misinterpreted hers. If looks could kill, you would be a dead man."

Sanjay had no doubt about that, and the thought actually bothered him. He slammed the glass down on the table, the whisky sloshing over the side, leaving a small puddle. Sanjay lost his temper and pushed Abhinav. "Stop asking me stupid questions and leave Trisha alone, you fucking moron. You have already ruined me once. And now you want to fight over a slutty model."

"Hold your tongue Sanjay! If I could, I would take away everything from you. Because it's all mine. I know you've stolen away a lot of money from the company of which fifty percent was rightfully mine. So I am going to take whatever I can from you. Even if it is your slutty model." Abhinav grunted.

"You are not going to get Trisha." Sanjay snapped. "She is mine and she is not going to come to you."

Abhinav looked amused as he nudged Sanjay. "These models are all the same, Sanjay. You've just got to tell them you can get them into a movie and they open their legs without you even asking. I am going to have an all night bash with her and let you know how I felt." He gave Sanjay a vicious smile and walked away.

Sanjay was beginning to dislike Abhinav Deo more and more.

Just then, the lights in the room were dimmed and a spotlight was focused on a mock stage set up at one end of the room with the bathroom and shower panel setup hidden behind the red velvet curtains. Manoj Bhatt was standing poised at a microphone. As soon as the babble died down he launched into a lengthy speech about Lasense lingerie and its designs. He knew how to promote the products to the journalists and made a simple range of lingerie sound like the next bedroom fashion trend. At the end of his speech there was a polite applause, after which he stood to one side and said, "And now I would like to show you the television commercial live in front of your eyes enacted by our talented model Miss Trisha Mehra herself!"

The red curtains were drawn back, and there was Trisha, standing just outside the shower panel, a little wet, with her glossy hair clinging to her shoulders. She was wearing nothing but deep red coloured lingerie. Sanjay felt a rush of stimulation inside his body.

Bharti stared blankly into space, her thoughts on the night before.

When Trisha finished enacting the commercial, there was a hearty applause from the men and a few jealous titters from the women. Then the curtains were drawn and the Lasense marketing head appeared at the microphone with more to say.

Sanjay saw his wife busy at the bar with some guests. He excused himself and made his way behind the stage to the green room. The green room had three wardrobes, one in the centre that held all the production attire and two not quite as large on each end. They appeared to be covered with a similar laminate as the wall paper, blending into the wall almost perfectly. The centre wardrobe divided the room into two sections, a kitchen and a small eating area on one side and a waiting room-type area on the other.

Large overstuffed chairs and sofas in shades of burgundy and green filled the waiting room, while the kitchen offered a table and two chairs as well as cabinets filled with snacks for the production staff. Four mirrors took up the opposite wall.

Trisha was patting herself dry with a towel in front of the mirrored wall and her dress and shoes were scattered around in her usual untidy style. She was wearing the dark red lingerie, which was clinging to her curvaceous body as it was completely wet. Sanjay felt his manhood rise.

She looked at him wearily. "What now?"

He walked over to her and put his hands on her shoulders. "I'm sorry," he said. "I won't ask you any more questions. You can live your life the way you want to. I will not boss you around." He lied shamelessly. It was more about ensuring that she didn't go away to Abhinav. He just couldn't see Abhinav win from him.

She threw him her wide-eyed look. "I can't believe it's Mr. Sanjay Kapoor talking so politely to me! Where is your obsession? Your arrogance? Tell me!"

"I promise you Trisha. I missed you and I am better off with you than with my unanswered questions."

She smiled and snaked her arms around his neck. Bringing Abhinav to the party was a good idea, after all. She had learnt to manage Sanjay well and she felt proud about it. "All right, you're forgiven Mr. Sanjay. But you—"

He silenced her the only way he could. With his mouth.

She cried out against his lips, trying to curl away from him. He moved closer, tightened his grip on her wrists and kissed her harder. She was active now, eating into his mouth, her heart racing against his.

Reality blurred. He captured both her wrists in one hand and cupped her face with the other. He then changed the angle of the kiss and nipped at her bottom lip. When she cried out at the tiny pain, he used the moment to slip his tongue into her mouth.

She gasped. And then, she made a weak whisper of sound. The sound a girl makes when she gives herself to her man. Sanjay let go of her wrists and thrust his hands into her hair. He tilted her face up to his and he took the kiss deeper, deeper, deeper...

They stared at each other for a long minute, both breathing hard. Then, slowly, still holding her hands, Sanjay took a step back and placed his hands on her shoulders. Her body was still wet as he put his hands in the top of her lingerie and slowly peeled it down. "Not here, my darling," she whispered. "Someone might come in. Anyone can come into the green room; we are in the middle of a launch party Sanjay!" she whimpered.

"I couldn't care less. In fact, that is giving me a real high. Making love to you secretly in a public place. I want you, Trisha," he whispered against her parted lips, his tongue softly tracing. "And I know you want me inside you as badly as I want to be there. Filling you, driving into you over and over. Making you scream just like last time."

She swallowed, her breaths changing to pants. "What kind of fantasy is this Sanjay? Making love in a public place? Just when I thought you were getting boring, you came out with a really wild idea." She moaned at the very thought. "So? Are you going to take me here? In the middle of this green room?"

"Maybe," he purred and then covered her mouth with his again, her taste racing through him.

Her arms lifted around his neck, her fingers dived into his hair, holding him closer. Grabbing her hips with both hands, he lifted her and then set her on top of the table. It was the perfect position for him to slide between her splayed thighs and press his aching manhood right inside her. Her heat singed him even through his clothes; something he desperately wanted to get rid of.

He pressed into her and swallowed her moan of pleasure. He could make her come here. He wanted to.

The remote sound of laughter of the crowd outside the green room drifted through to Sanjay which reminded him of his wife standing outside in the party. Trisha pulled her mouth from his, "I'm soon going to fulfil your fantasy of having me in a public place," she whispered.

"Is that a promise?"

"I promise I will make you come, in public. It will be a night you will never forget."

Laughter and squeals echoed from outside and somebody hurled against the door. They both froze. Trisha separated herself completely from Sanjay and stepped on to the couch to wear her red dress.

God, how much time had passed? Too much, Sanjay realized, risking a glance at the clock, stunned to realize nearly ten minutes had passed since he had followed her into the green room. Ten minutes spent lost in her arms, and lost in her kisses.

Slowly, he straightened, meeting her eyes, lifting his hand as he lowered his forehead to hers and damned himself to hell. There was no way he could stay away from her, not when she kissed him like that, not when she melted against him, not when she came in his arms like she had been made for his touch alone. Drawing back, he stared at her, laying one hand along her cheek.

"Let's meet again at your place, Trisha?" he asked again.

She nodded silently, pausing briefly to adjust her dress, before stepping past him.

The door closed gently behind her, leaving Sanjay to stare at the walls adorned with clothes for the models and cosmetics piled on the dressing table. He shrugged his suit jacket back into place, automatically adjusting it to hide his manhood as he ran his hands down his face before dipping them into his pockets.

How had this happened? How had he succumbed to her? Was he in love with her? Or was it just lust?

Sanjay returned to the gathering and mixed with the crowd. He grabbed a drink and started talking to the clients. He stealthily looked around for Bharti and found her seated at the bar, talking to the same journalist who she had been with earlier. He took a deep breath of relief.

"I'd like you to meet Shirish Roy, a friend of mine from Delhi. Shirish's here to direct the new Abhinav Deo movie," the reporter said, with a sparkle in her eyes.

"Really," said Bharti. "How interesting! I met the model of this advertisement earlier this evening… She is going to be the actress in this movie, I heard. I would have checked it with Abhinav, but you know, these days my husband is not on good terms with him."

Shirish raised a quizzical eyebrow. "That sounds interesting." He spoke with a short, razor-sharp tone. "We haven't even done the casting for the movie and someone has already declared herself the lead actress. Strange things happen in Mumbai, I must say."

Bharti smiled. "I suppose she's suffering from delusions."

"What's the name of that model, anyway?" Shirish asked.

Bharti frowned. "I can't really remember. My husband will know, she just did this lingerie commercial for his company."

Just then, Sanjay arrived. He seemed to be in a very good mood. He put his arm around Bharti and smiled at her.

"Sweetheart," Bharti interrupted him, "What was the name of that little girl who was doing the Lasense thing?"

"What?" he asked, feeling guilty instantaneously. "Why do you want to know her name?"

Bharti looked at him oddly, or maybe he thought she did. "Do I need to have a reason for asking you her name?" she asked.

He felt the tension build in the short silence that followed, and then he laughed weakly and said, "Of course not. It's Trisha Mehra. Why, what happened?"

Shirish shook his head. "I have never heard of her."

"What's happening? Did I miss something?" questioned Sanjay.

"Well," said Bharti, "Do you remember she said she was going to be the lead actress in the new movie that your ex-partner Abhinav is producing? Shirish is directing it. I thought he would know about her. Anyway, apparently she isn't in that movie."

"She didn't say she was in it at all," said Sanjay coldly. "She said she had been to see Abhinav Deo and he liked her, that's all. That's how these models talk. That's how they spread rumours and gain publicity."

Shirish laughed. "That accounts for the confusion. Abhinav is always seeing these aspiring actresses and stringing them along. Abhinav just puts up a big casting month and enjoys seeing them; it makes him happy. Pardon me but sometimes he likes to see two to three girls at a time too."

Sanjay scowled at him. "It makes him happy, but what about the girls whose hopes he builds up?" His hatred was evident in his words.

Shirish shrugged. "That's show business. Most of them know how it works, and the ones that don't soon learn the rules of the trade. I know you have had a bad past with Abhinav, but that was long ago, and I think you should let it go." He patted Sanjay's shoulder. "We all are part of the same industry and we should be professional with each other."

Bharti nodded at his comment. "It was a good time when you both worked together. I remember him being a big support. At least you had the time to come home every day."

Sanjay nodded to her comment. He was in no mood to listen to either Bharti or Shirish.

"I think I need a drink" Shirish stood up. "How about you, Mrs. Kapoor?"

"Please call me Bharti. I'd love a gin and tonic."

Sanjay looked at his watch. It was 1.30 a.m. Trisha would be safely in bed. She had promised that she was going straight back home. He wondered if he could call her, but then decided it was too late. He didn't want to wake her, and anyway there was little chance of making a phone call with Bharti around.

Shirish returned with the drinks. Bharti and Shirish hit it off very well. Shirish told her about all the advertising films that he had done for Sanjay's company in the past and how he enjoyed working with both him and Abhinav. Finally he said to Sanjay, "I must say, you are a very lucky man. Your wife is stunning and smart, quite a combination."

Sanjay smiled at his comment. He had a long lasting professional relation with Shirish as they had worked together on many advertising films. While Sanjay had split up with Abhinav, he still worked with Shirish as he was an established director.

Bharti was beginning to feel much better, her headache had disappeared, and she had had just enough to drink to take away any weariness. She had pushed Ankit to the back of her mind and was enjoying talking to Shirish.

Around half an hour later, Bharti said stifling a yawn, "I think we better get going. I'm absolutely tired."

No one else in the party seemed interested in leaving, so they said their good-byes. At last they were alone. Bharti leaned back in the car and closed her eyes. Sanjay said, not really meaning it, "You and Shirish were getting very friendly."

She opened her eyes. "Not more than you and that trampy lingerie model."

He shot her a dark look. "I didn't even talk to her. I don't know what you mean."

"Oh Sanjay, really!" She sighed. "You didn't even talk to her? You went pale when I asked her name." She paused, then added inquiringly, "Have you ever taken her out?"

He stared furiously at the road ahead. "That is a preposterous question!"

"I just wondered. You seemed so interested in her and kept getting in little huddles with her."

"She works for our company. I was just trying to see that the launch went off smoothly, that's all."

"I know how much you are interested in your work. Had you given even fifty percent of your serious focus to the business, it wouldn't have been in such losses. My dad funded your business and helped you stand on your feet. But you screwed that up too."

"Bharti—"

"You listen to me tonight, Mr. Sanjay Kapoor. You lost all my father's money and you cheated your partner. And though I know that you hardly get any work, you are always busy. There are always clients pouring in. Sometimes I wonder if you work so hard, then where does the money disappear?"

Sanjay had no intent to answer these questions. He knew where the money was. He knew he could make a sale and exit anytime. He knew the business was in trouble, not him. The only trouble was that he was still thinking about Trisha. They lapsed into silence. He switched the car stereo on. He was in no mood to listen to her blabber.

Bharti felt weak. She could see her marriage shattering into pieces. "Darling," Bharti said quickly, though tentatively, "What's wrong?"

"What do you mean, what's wrong?" replied Sanjay.

"I mean, what's wrong with us? What's happening to us? Why all of a sudden are we so far apart from each other?"

He turned off the stereo. "I don't think we are so far apart. Everything is as it should be." His tone was indifferent. Bharti was nothing but a show piece in his life which made him look good in social functions.

She looked out of the car window. They were driving near a park, and the trees looked dark and gloomy as they sped past them. "It's amusing, Sanjay. This must have begun to happen to us for years, and yet neither of us realized it; neither of us tried to improve the situation. We just meet for an hour a day without talking about what's happening in our lives. We have become like the tracks of a train; we are together but we never meet. The only thing we have in common is that we stay in the same house and sleep on the same bed."

"I think you're really exhausted and drunk and that's why talking loads of crap. There is nothing wrong. Each relation has an initial peak and then it stabilizes at a level. What has happened to you tonight?"

"Loads of crap?" she repeated his words. "Is that how you talk to your wife? Is that what you think I am? A piece of crap?" Tears started to roll silently down her cheeks. "When did you last sit with me and ask me about my day? When did you last hug me? When did you come back home and kiss me? And when did you really want to make love to me? Answer me Sanjay!"

"Oh, so that's what this conversation is all about."

She tried to keep her tears under control. "No, that's not what this is about, but it's a part of it. I feel lonely even after being in a relationship with you. You are never there. I keep waiting for you and then later get a small message from you that you won't be able to come."

He pulled the car onto the side of the road and stopped. Then he turned around to face her. What could he say? That he didn't find her interesting anymore? That Trisha was a much better lay? She was actually correct; really, they were far apart from each other. "What do you want me to say?" he said, realizing he had no more lies that he could say to make this right. Bharti had exploded like a volcano and he wasn't enjoying being trapped with her.

"Do you remember the first year of our marriage, Sanjay? Everything was great. We were in love with each other. Even though there was lots of work in your office, you made an effort to come home or take me out for a date. We talked to each other, we listened to each other and we made sweet love for hours," she said.

She looked into his eyes. Looking into his eyes was like looking into a glacier. No softness and no sentiment at all. Yes, he remembered the good times. He remembered the hot amazing pleasurable nights with Bharti...the sexy and young Bharti, who awoke all sorts of desires and needs in him. "Yes, I remember the first year of our marriage," he said inaudibly.

"Why can't things be like they were then?" She looked at him.

"Bharti, we have been together for years now. There are ups and downs in romance too. Like I said, every relation grows exponentially and reaches a peak. We were at our peak a few years back. Everything doesn't stay where it was, you know." His voice was cool but insulting.

"Yes, I know," she said. *Ankit makes me feel wanted. He makes me feel desirable and I feel that I am much younger.*

Sanjay said. "We'd better be getting home. I need to get to the office early in the morning," he said laconically.

"You will never change Sanjay," she said coldly. "Arrogant and impossible and so damn sure of yourself." *Why are you still worried about going to office? Are you even listening to me? Why don't you kiss me now? Why don't you make love to me right now in the car? Why don't you make me feel that you need me in your life?*

They drove home in an uncomfortable silence, both realizing that there was more unsaid than said. The dam of marriage had broken long ago; this was just the arrival of the storm.

The house seemed cold and gloomy. Sanjay went to the bathroom while Bharti pulled on a pair of white cotton pajamas, yanked a pale gray T-shirt over her head and settled into the bed. She wondered if because of their argument about not making love, he would want to make love to her tonight.

She was wrong. He didn't. He returned from the bathroom, got into bed and appeared to go straight off to sleep without wishing her good night.

She lay there annoyed and disturbed. *I tried to save our marriage. I really tried to make him understand that we were drifting apart. But he doesn't seem to care about what's happening to us.*

◆

The next morning, Sanjay's thoughts were still on Trisha as he woke up. He hadn't stopped thinking about the fantasy they had discussed in the green room. When he had kissed her, he wasn't sure if she'd kiss him back, nor had he the faintest notion how quickly things would heat up between them. He'd fallen asleep dreaming about the fantasy of making love to her in a public place secretly, in a dark private area where they could overhear the chatter of the people in the party. Oh that would be thrilling, he thought. But it was a fantasy best played in a dream and nearly impossible in real life.

He looked around. It was a rainy morning. Sanjay turned his face up toward the sky from his living room window and sighed. The trees were so tall and thick he barely saw the sky peeking out between the tips of the branches, which made the room floor dark and cold. The blue had been replaced by dark gray clouds that obscured the tips of the trees. Sanjay could feel the darkness of the clouds in his relationship with his wife.

He opened the window and the cool wind hit against his cheeks, the smell of damp dirt and dead leaves mingled in the breeze tickled his nose, which reminded him of the time he had made love to Trisha in his car on a rainy day. He couldn't get enough of her, and that was not a good thing. Forcing his thoughts away from her, he decided to get ready for his office.

He brushed, shaved, showered, and got ready without disturbing Bharti. He ate breakfast at the glass table, read the newspaper along with it and drank orange juice to hydrate him after the long drinking session he had yesterday. Over the last couple of days, he couldn't seem to get Trisha out of his mind. He thought that maybe if he saw her again, he could figure out what it was about her that had him so intrigued. She was beautiful, that was for certain, but it was more than that. Looking down at his glass, he realized it was empty.

Bharti awoke shortly after. The morning passed in a flurry of domesticity and she got no time to think about Sanjay, or Ankit for that matter. There was no message from Ankit.

In the evening, after finishing some planned household chores and a hot water bubble bath, she picked up the phone to call Sanjay, only to realize that there was a missed call from Shirish Roy. She decided to call him in a few minutes and first called Sanjay. He didn't pick up the call so she sent him a message to call her as soon as he could. Then she returned Shirish Roy's call.

"Hi."

"Hi Shirish. How are you? I just saw your missed call so I called back."

"Well, I am doing good and was wondering if you and Sanjay could join me for dinner tomorrow night?" he said. "It will be great if you both can come home as I am throwing a small party."

"I'll have to check with Sanjay and get back to you on this," Bharti replied.

It was a short conversation. Bharti looked up at her mobile screen and checked for Sanjay's message or missed call. None.

Sanjay didn't call until past seven. "I'll be late," he said in a hurried tone.

"How late?" Bharti asked.

"I don't know, probably around twelve."

"Where do you have to go?"

His voice was angry. "What is this? Why are you asking me so many details? I told you I have some work to do."

She replied coldly. "I think I have the right to know the details of why you're going to be late and what work are you busy in."

There was a silence, then, "I'm sorry, of course you do. I'm exhausted, I suppose. I shouldn't have been rude. Actually, I've got a late meeting with Manoj to catch up on the schedule of our next campaign." Sanjay cooked up a story.

"Why don't you bring him home and have your meeting over dinner? I will cook some great food."

"No, it's all right. I do not want you to get into unnecessary trouble. We'll order something and have a working dinner."

"I'll wait for you Sanjay."

"Please don't wait up. I don't know when the work might finish. Bye."

"Bye." She hung up and yawned.

Just then, she realized that she had forgotten to ask about the dinner invite from Shirish Roy. Quickly, she picked up her iPhone and dialled back Sanjay's mobile. It was unreachable. So she called his direct line at the office. It rang and rang, but there was no reply. She hung up and looked in her mobile's phone book for Manoj's number. Sometimes Sanjay's phone was unreachable due to poor network. When she dialled Manoj's number, some female picked up. His wife, she said.

"I'm sorry to bother you," said Bharti, "but I just wanted to talk to Manoj."

"Yes, sure," said his wife, sounding somewhat surprised to get a call from her. "But he is in the bathroom right now. We are about to leave for a movie. I will ask him to call you as soon as he is ready."

Now it was Bharti's turn to sound surprised. "But isn't he working late with Sanjay tonight for the next campaign's production schedule or something like that?"

"No, I don't think so. I have the movie tickets in my hand," she replied.

"Oh," said Bharti quietly, embarrassed. She didn't want to make a fool of herself and discuss her personal issues with her. "I must have made a mistake then. I am really sorry to bother you. Bye." Bharti speedily cut off the call.

She was shocked. So all this while Sanjay had been lying to her about late night meetings. Why was he lying? How long had he been lying? And why was it only now, when she herself had been disloyal, that she had to find out? It was obviously because of another female in his life!

She felt really stupid for not realizing that Sanjay was being adulterous right under her nose. That is why he had no interest in her. That is why he frequently came home late and travelled a lot on business trips. It all just tied in. She realized that because there was an emotional and physical void in her life, she was subconsciously attracted to Ankit. She felt cheated and didn't know what to do. Tears seemed gloomily and pointlessly close.

If things had been all right with Sanjay and me, then I would never have looked twice at Ankit.

All Bharti could do was sulk at her situation. She summoned up some courage and tried to stop crying. Where was that going to get her? She went into the bathroom and washed her face, then stared at her reflection in the mirror. The tears just wouldn't stop. She didn't know what to do next. She knew she couldn't live in the hope of sitting around waiting for Sanjay to finally come home, fresh from the arms of some slut. She had no one to call. After marriage, she had gradually lost touch with all her close friends as most of them had got busy in their lives. She thought of calling her mother, but to confide in her would be a big risk as she was old and had heart problems. When she could think of no one to call, she decided to call Ankit.

He answered immediately. "Hello."

She got cold feet and froze, not saying anything. Then she hung up in panic. She didn't know what she was doing. He called back at once.

"Listen Bharti! Don't hang up. I've been waiting for you to call me."

"If that is true, why didn't you call me till now?"

"I didn't want to be an obstacle in your personal life. I wasn't sure about the right time to call you. I didn't know when your husband was around or away from you. My call could have disrupted your personal life and I didn't want to do anything that would hurt you."

She smiled at his sweet comment. He was considerate and mature in his own way.

"What if I had never called back?"

"I knew you would call. We have something in between us. I am sure you agree. I want to see you. Can you come over?"

"When?" she muttered weakly.

"How about right now?"

"I don't know. I am not sure if I can do that."

"Please, I need to talk to you."

"Well, all right. I'll be there in sometime." Bharti was keen to meet him.

"Great." He gave her the address in case she had forgotten it.

She hurriedly searched in her closet for the right clothes, until she spotted a blue silk top with a sexy oval deep neck and white lowers to go with it. She wore the simplest jewellery: a pearl necklace with a flash of gleam at the ears. She quickly strapped the silver sandals, and a bag to match with a glittering buckle to mirror the earrings. She wanted to look good even though she felt miserable inside.

And then the makeup…how did you look like a lady who wanted to be in the arms of a stranger? She settled on smoky eyes with a more nude, not-so-obvious lip gloss. Sleek hair. No make-up anywhere else, except to cover her tear-struck face. She thought the look was dead-on-smouldering but not trashy, sensual but not flashy-beautiful, elegant, and sexy – everything she'd felt in the last ten minutes.

She locked the house and drove the distance to where he lived. It was an old high rise building with several flats. She took the lift and reached the fifth floor and stepped out and searched for the correct flat.

He answered her knock immediately.

"So," he murmured.

"Charming place." She didn't know what else to say.

"Thank you."

"I don't really know what I'm doing here," she blurted.

He took her by the hand and led her inside. "You look lovely. I've been going crazy waiting for you to call me."

"Why didn't you call me Ankit?"

"Like I said earlier, I understand that you are married. I was waiting for you to take the next step or chose to stay out of this relationship. I wanted to give you all the time for making the right decision. And I am glad you did."

He made her feel very young and wanted. "I know nothing about you," she murmured.

With an inward groan, she couldn't help but admire how nice he looked. He wore a blue denim shirt unbuttoned at the neck. The sleeves were rolled up and showed off muscular forearms. The lack of hair on his chest made his skin look smooth and her fingers itched to skim over that softness, to feel the warm texture of his flesh beneath their tips. The jeans hugged his hips and thighs and she had to bite back the sigh that threatened to slip out.

With the clearing of his throat, her eyes snapped back to his and she tried to control her thundering heart. He raised an eyebrow and his mouth spread in a suggestive grin. He looked devilish and seductive and oh so dangerous. "You're always saying that," he said.

They were standing in a small room with white walls with a lot of beautiful framed photographs. The only furniture was a wooden dining table, piled high with CDs, utensils, belts and possibly everything. She sat on the couch, and he offered her gin and tonic. He fixed her drink, then put on the music and sat beside her on the couch.

"About that night," she began uncertainly, "I think what happened should never have happened. Actually I had a fight with my husband that night and drank a lot and landed up with you."

He took her hand. "So you mean that it was a one night stand that you regret?

"No Ankit, I didn't mean that—"

"I think what happened that night had to happen, and I am glad it did. It means a lot to me. I am lucky to have you in my life. I don't think you regretted that night because if you did, you wouldn't have come to me again." He smiled at her and held out a small velvet case.

She took another gulp of her gin. "What is this?"

He smiled. "It's nothing much. Have a look. I got it for you."

She opened the small velvet box and saw a small gold pendant in the shape of a heart. She took it out and admired it. It was small and she knew it wouldn't be too expensive. But she knew it was too expensive for Ankit.

"I can't take it. I just can't. You don't have to spend money on me." Bharti was feeling elated at his sweet gesture but she didn't want Ankit to spend money as she knew that he was not too rich.

"It's not too much." He explained. "I work at Ethos Jewellers as a Sales Manager. In the last few days, I have crossed my monthly target. I just received an incentive in the form of gift vouchers and I thought I should buy this pendant for you." He grinned. "After all, I have achieved this target because of you."

"Because of me?" she wondered.

"Yes, my boss says I am under good influence and tremendously happy these days."

She hesitated and then rushed on. "I just didn't want to leave you with the wrong impression of me. Neither that day. Nor today."

"You left me with a beautiful impression; your perfume was all over my bed, and the smell of your body in my senses, and the way you cried out when you came…" He reached over for her. "And I am sure you will not leave me with a wrong impression even today." Their mouths met and she was lost.

She let him tip her head back and continue to rain kisses over the bare flesh of her neck. She also let him slip her top over her head and loosen the clasp of her bra. It fell to the floor unnoticed as Ankit cupped her breasts in his hands, leaning back to study the sight of his hands on her pale flesh. The rounded globes of her breasts were silky soft, her nipples puckering and drawing tight as he rolled each one between his finger and thumb, before lowering his head to take one reddened tip into his mouth. His hands trailed lower, over her narrow ribcage, over the indent of her waist before settling on the softly rounded curve of her hips. Grasping one firmly curved ass cheek in his hand, he dragged her lower body against his as he feasted on her sweet, hot nipples.

He kissed his way back up to her neck before leaning back to stare at her with hot, hungry eyes. His fingers left her aching nipples to stroke the underside and outer curve of her breasts while he murmured, "You've got such pretty breasts. And you taste so good."

God, his touch made her feel wanted. She had not felt like this in a long time. This was what mattered. This moment. Now.

Taking her mouth in another drugging, incredible kiss, he walked her backward until she came up against the wall. Pinning her there, he lifted her hips until she locked her legs around him. Groaning, he buried his face in her neck.

Her scent rose to haunt him, lovable and erotic, naive and appealing. He lowered his head and gently bit the underside of one breast as he ground himself against the heat between her legs. He snarled in disappointment at the cloth that separated them and reached for the zipper of her lowers, jerking them open and down in two quick actions. Bharti fell back against the wall, her head whirling dizzily as Ankit knelt in front of her and pulled her lowers completely off and away, before he leaned forward, nuzzling the front panel of her panties momentarily before he rose and grabbed her hips again, fitting himself into the notch between her thighs and rocking against her.

Through the heavy denim, Bharti could feel his manhood, hard and long, as he thrust against her silk covered flesh. A weak moan rose in the air before dying away into the silence. A sharp gasp. Quivering with heavy breaths, a weak, moaning whimper escaped her as Ankit thrust his fingers past the silky barrier of her panties, searching in on the delights they hid. His fingers slid efficiently across her wet flesh, plummeting deeply into her hungering body. She closed around him, tight and wet, exceptionally sweet.

Her head was thrown back, her cheeks glowing, her mouth swollen. He didn't want to think, didn't want to do anything other than taste this woman, to bury himself inside her. He leaned down and captured her mouth in a tender kiss that stole her breath away. She lifted her arms around his neck, returning his kiss with all the passion and love she felt in her heart. With her arms wrapped tight around him and her legs holding his waist, he lifted her up and took her towards the bed.

The warmth of his body seeped into hers more with every step he took, finally to create a stark contrast to the cool sheet beneath her. He moved downward, his teeth tugging at her nipples. She inhaled sharply at the sensations his touch produced. Her whole body was on fire.

"You have such a delicious body, Bharti," he sighed against the flesh of her stomach.

Going lower on his knees, he drew her panties down her long, sleekly muscled thighs, stroking one long narrow foot as he spread her legs. Leaning forward, he used his tongue, drawing it up near her entrance in one long stroke. She shrieked, tried to pull him away from her core. "Let me," he said, pulling away long enough to take her hands and pin them down to her sides. "God, you're sweet."

His lips travelled lower until they touched the soft skin just above her vertical entrance. Her breathing amplified. Oh God. She wanted him to touch her there, to lick her and ease the ache that was quickly building to an inferno. He inhaled and grinned. "Hmm, I wonder if you taste as good as you smell."

He gave gentle, nuzzling kisses near her thighs while one hand lazily stroked her. She watched, captivated by his actions and the provoking effect they had on her.

"You like that?" he mumbled and, with his palms, spread her legs wider.

"Ankit," she whimpered as his tongue lightly licked her up.

One finger slid deep in her while his tongue mischievously circled her, sending sharp sparks of pleasure over every inch of her flesh. Without warning, he moved another finger inside. She stiffened at the invasion, her eyes rolling back as the bite of pain quickly morphed to blinding satisfaction. He pushed the fingers deeper, as his tongue tenderly licked her. With scissor like movements, he teased her, igniting a desire she never imagined existed.

She gasped, her breath coming out in pants as he slowly amplified the rhythm and force. She closed her eyes, her hips moving in time with his hand. She didn't know what he was doing, what spot he was rubbing against, but the sensation was hard to believe. It kept building, getting stronger. He pulled away momentarily to stare at her sex before glancing up at her. "God, you're good. I could eat you for hours," he mumbled before diving for her again.

"You're killing me." She sighed.

"Ah, baby. I haven't even started yet."

He rose, planting hot, sharp kisses against her belly.

"Now," he mumbled, and he once again lifted her hips and positioned himself between her legs. He brushed against the damp triangle between her legs, hot, smooth and hard. She gasped, arching back as he slid once, twice, three times against her. On the fourth pass, she cried out as waves of pleasure washed over her, emanating outward from the centre of her body.

He chuckled, and lowered his head to purr in her ear, "Like that? I hope you like that. And I hope you're going to like it even more when I'm deep inside you. You're so hot!"

She gasped and cried out a second time as he slid inside, thrusting deep, forcing himself through her channel. As Ankit moved further inside her, she moaned in mindless pleasure. "Shh," he murmured in her ear, "Relax, honey. Just relax, and enjoy," he said softly, withdrawing just a little before sliding in again. "You're fine. Damn more than fine."

Ankit shifted his grip until one arm was wrapped beneath her buttocks. He nudged himself in a little further, groaning as she clamped around him tighter, hot wet silk. He raised his head, found her mouth without opening his eyes. She was hot and wet and ready for him. She wanted him every bit as much as he wanted her. He bit sharply at her lip and her eyes flew open, screaming a little, before catching her breath, arching up as he withdrew and plunged back into the wet, silky-smooth depths of her. Her flesh writhed convulsively around him, forcing Ankit to grit his teeth against his body's impulses.

Eyes closed, face buried against her neck, Ankit rocked against her, gently rotating his hips, adjusting his thrusts so that he brushed against sensitized flesh every time he moved. She was trembling against him, around him. Each breath she took tightened her muscles in a slow, pleasing caress around his manhood. He pulled out a little, pushed in, moaning helplessly when it set her muscles to writhing, and her inner walls to clinging around his length. They rocked together like lovers. He kissed her juicy lips, stroking her with his tongue, tasting himself on her, tasting their scent, their sex on her lips and deep in her mouth.

The feel of him between her legs was intense. He was so long and strong, she felt as if he was her centre and she was rolling around it and over it. She rubbed it and bounced on it and cradled it deeply and lustfully between her legs, and she never wanted him to withdraw from her.

He angled his hips up, thrusting into her in an unanticipated tight thrust that caught her just as her body craved, sending her into a rocketing orgasm that was a series of spiky, hard explosions of pleasure.

"You are amazing." His voice was raw with want and pleasure.

"Yessss," as he pumped her between her legs. "Oh, yesss." And she went insane, seduced by the feel of his fingers on her hips, the feelings he provoked, the arousing sounds he whispered in her ear, the feel of his tongue licking the curve of her neck. He held her bottom tight; he thrust at her body in short, hard, piston-like bursts, grunting in rhythm with his movements. One-two-three-four…Bharti found herself counting…two-three-four…coming… She could feel him growing deep inside her, getting harder and hotter. He sat there, still grasping her buttocks, still embedded, hard as a tree trunk. And then, the firecracker of an orgasm caught her by surprise. Her heart started pounding. The moment was here suddenly, sooner than she expected it. Hot lights exploded all over her body, inside her body, and she recklessly wrung every last flash point of pleasure from his thrusting manhood. Her body felt brittle with emotions that would crack wide open if she moved. She went very still, her heart thumping like a drum.

Ankit swallowed her gasping scream with his mouth, felt the woman convulse around him as he reached a soaring climax himself. Her body aching and her mouth swollen from the rough kisses, Bharti lay staring at the ceiling in Ankit's room. What had she done? Yet again! Quickly, Bharti shoved the thought from her mind. He was young and full of strength, and this time she was almost sober and couldn't blame it on the alcohol. His whole attempt seemed to be to try to please her. They made love for a long time, and it was beyond all boundaries. Afterward they lay and talked. She felt so peaceful and protected by him. He listened quietly while she told him about Sanjay and his indifference toward her. She told him everything about her life. They drank some gin and tonic and she found out about him too.

Ankit's mother was dead and his father, a retired government officer, lived in Delhi. He told her about his ex-girlfriend. "She was perfectly lovely. She always wore attractive clothes, and when she spoke, she said only correct things. We were deeply in love and our parents had met each other to finalize our marriage. On the day of the wedding, she didn't turn up. I was so shocked. I later came to know that she hooked up with the son of a rich business man. I think she wanted a guy with a lot of money. That day I realized that even after being in love for so many years, how immature can young girls be," he said.

"Do you still think about her?" questioned Bharti.

"The idea of marrying a woman like her – of sharing the rest of my life with someone so obsessed with appearance, status, and money – makes my skin crawl. I thank God that I was saved," he said moodily. "The only thing that I remember is that she was really immature and so are all the other young girls that I have met. They don't know what they want and it freaks me out."

"I think I'm all right for you because I'm married?" she guessed.

"I think it's not about being married. It's about being mature."

They lay in silence for a while, both mulling over their problems. She leaned over and kissed him lightly on the forehead. After a while she looked at her watch, and seeing that it was past eleven, she said, "Look, I need to go. Sanjay's going to be home anytime now."

"Why don't you stay the night?" he mumbled.

"I'd like to, but I just need to be there when he gets home. He knows I never stay out, so I don't want him to get worried unnecessarily."

"It's funny, isn't it," Ankit said. "All the young girls that I have met want me, but they can't get me. I want you, and I can't get you." He put on a high tone voice. "You know, Bharti, you're the first female since my marriage broke, whom I've asked to stay the night…and you say no."

His eyes followed the slight swaying of her hips as she walked towards the dressing table. Her thigh muscles rippled as she bent down to pick up the hair brush from the table. His manhood thickened uncomfortably. Damn, the woman could set his blood on fire without even trying at all. She dressed slowly as Ankit lay lazily back in bed watching her.

Ankit continued to watch Bharti getting ready in front of the mirror. Her hair fell down her back in loose curls, the soft lights from above made her hair shine. Her clothes hugged her firm behind, accentuating every dip and curve.

She thought he was watching her and she turned around suddenly. Their gazes locked, and she squirmed beneath his heated stare. He broke eye contact first and raked his gaze over her in a way that made her feel bare. Turning away, she tried to give her full attention to her reflection in the mirror. She was surprised at the fact that her body reacted this way to his presence. It was as if she had no control over it. She didn't want this magnetism to him, and the aggravation within that came out as a hot desire for him.

Closing her eyes with a sigh, she put her forehead to the glass. Her hands shook slightly as she brushed her hair away from her face. A lump formed in her throat, and she swallowed hard to get rid of her burning desire. Eventually, she was ready to go back home.

"When am I going to see you again?" he asked.

"I am not sure."

"Tomorrow?"

"I am not sure, Ankit. It's very difficult for me to make plans."

"Now that we have come so close, you can't leave without telling me when. I will miss you."

"I'll call you," she said.

He kissed her long and hard, and she set off on her way home. It was past midnight when she reached. She was worried that Sanjay might reach before her.

Sanjay was very good at telling lies to his wife. So he had cooked up a false story about meeting Manoj thinking that he would spend some warm and cozy time with the hot Trisha. But he had dialled her number many times and listened to her ringtone *"Tonight's gonna be a good good night."* Well, the night was not as good as it was supposed to be.

He drove around for a few minutes and then stopped on the side. This girl had made him go crazy. He dialled the number and listened to it ring, but no one answered, so he dialled again; but still got no reply. He let it ring for a long time, but there was no answer. At last he reached the obvious conclusion that she was either too drunk or too deeply asleep to be disturbed.

He was desperate to meet her. He switched the ignition on and with a sudden flash of decision drove to where she lived. He rang the doorbell, but there was no answer.

"Slut!" he mumbled to himself.

He hung around outside for a while, and kept trying her mobile. He imagined her with Abhinav Deo. Her smooth, beautiful body crushed to his, going through the motions of love-making which she practiced so expertly. He could almost hear her small delicate cries of pleasure, her little moans, and the way she garbled rudimentary words in a low, deep voice.

He was angry with himself for being so hung up about her. He couldn't seem to get Trisha out of his mind. She was like a drug and he was totally addicted to her.

After a few minutes, she finally answered her phone. The music was very loud in the background, and she sounded in high spirits. He listened to her voice saying "Hello," then a pause, then "Hello, why are you not speaking?" Then another longer pause, and then "Why have you called if you don't want to speak!" And the phone was disconnected by her.

Sanjay was furious. "How dare that bitch disconnect my phone call! She needs to be taught a lesson." He at once went to her main gate and started banging on the door.

She answered her front door and looked shocked to see him. She was wearing nothing but a large man-sized white shirt. As usual, she looked sharp enough to draw blood at all the right places.

"What a pleasant surprise!" she said. "Why were you not speaking on the phone? I kept saying hello hello!"

"I was shouting at the top of my voice," he said. "Either you were too drunk or the music was too loud for you to hear my voice," he barked loudly.

"But, why are you shouting? Just calm down." Trisha was completely drunk and couldn't figure out why Sanjay was jabbering so much.

He followed her into the living room. The music system seemed to be on full volume. A nearly empty bottle of vodka stood on the table.

"Want a drink?" she asked.

"Are you out of your mind? Since when have you been drinking? It's just 8 p.m. and the bottle seems to be empty!" he said sarcastically.

"Oh dear! Sorry daddy, I didn't know you look at your watch before you have a drink." she mumbled. She poured herself the remaining vodka from the bottle, lit a cigarette, and flopped down on the floor.

"Well, Sanjay, what brings you here?"

"I want to talk to you." He paced the room angrily, "I want to discuss lot of things with you."

She giggled. "Don't start off like my husband. I told you I wasn't tied to you. I warned you that you cannot tell me what to do. I do whatever I want, whenever I want, with whomsoever I want."

He shook his head at her in dismay. "I don't understand you. Sometimes you act like a fucking slut."

"We are both alike, Sanjay. Just because I am a girl you are calling me a slut. Even you have slept with many aspiring models! So that makes the two of us."

She rolled over on her stomach, taking a long drag of her cigarette, and blowing the smoke toward him. Then she said calmly, "I'm on the seventh heaven today, and no one can drag me down from there, not even you. So stop trying and enjoy the evening."

She rolled onto her back and stretched, the taut outline of her breasts appearing through her shirt. He felt the familiar hot desire creep up on him.

"Abhinav Deo has agreed to do a lot for me," she said breaking his trance.

"Sure, the only thing he is going to do, is you," said Sanjay mockingly.

Trisha could feel the derogatory undertones in his voice, but she swallowed it and tried to remain calm. She didn't want to spoil her evening. "In case you don't know, I'm being cast this week for his new film."

"He is just playing with you!" Sanjay said in a decidedly chilly tone.

"You're just envious baby, that's all. He can give me what you can't and that's why you can't take it," she reminded him tautly in a sharp voice that he had not done much for her.

"You're making a fool of yourself. I know Abhinav's style very well. This is his hobby, sleeping away with girls like you. I know him very well." Sanjay replied arrogantly in his I-know-it-all tone.

"Come on, Sanjay baby. I'm not a fool. I know the process. And if the process requires sleeping with some people, I am happy to do that. Trisha's mobile rang just at that moment. Trisha looked at the screen and reluctantly received the call.

"Hi," she said softly. She glanced quickly over to Sanjay. Like a suspicious husband, he immediately wondered who it was. "That will be great," she was saying. "What time works for you?" She looked back at Sanjay. "Sure, I will be there." She hung up.

"Who was that?" he asked, trying to keep his voice casual.

"Who was what?" she asked.

"Who was that on the phone?"

She hesitated for just a second too long before saying, "It was just another model. I met her at a party. She wants me to have dinner with her tomorrow."

"Don't lie to me. I am sure it was Abhinav Deo asking you for a night out," Sanjay said in a glaring tone.

Trisha completely lost her temper. "Don't try and act like my husband! I have told you so many times that I am not your slave. It's my life and I can do whatever I want. So just stop asking me questions!"

"Fine," said Sanjay and walked out of her apartment. Let this whore rot in hell. She was becoming too much of a pain in the ass. First, she didn't take his calls the entire day. On top of that, she had been to bed with Abhinav Deo. She was nothing but a slut, an easy lay. And in front of his eyes, she was lying to him to fix another date with Abhinav! This was too much. She could get lost. He was going home.

He roamed about the city, driving aimlessly for a few hours, and then finally decided to go home.

♦

Sanjay parked his car and walked towards the house. He saw Bharti unlocking the door and entering the house.

Sanjay followed her swiftly inside the house. "Where the hell have you been?" he demanded in an authoritative tone.

"I went to a movie. Where were you?" Bharti snapped.

"You know where I was. There are no movies so late in the night. So where have you been?" he asked suspiciously.

"I suppose you were in a late night meeting with Manoj," she said, ignoring his question.

"Yes, I had called you and informed you about that," he replied confidently.

"Well, if you were with him, then I was with him too. In the same meeting. You didn't see me?" she said sarcastically.

Dumbstruck, he stared at her blankly. "What the fuck are you talking about?"

"I was with Manoj as much as you were," she snapped.

"Are you out of your mind? Have you been drinking?" Sanjay replied with a touch of shock in his voice.

"No, Sanjay, I haven't been drinking. I called Manoj after speaking to you earlier, and his wife picked up and told me they were going out for a movie. So I wonder which meeting you have been to with Manoj when he was watching a movie with his wife!" Bharti was now screaming at the top of her voice.

He realized that he had been caught red-handed. But he was a sleazy bastard, always ready to cover his tracks. So he quickly tried to cook up a story. "Yes, there was a bit of confusion. We were both supposed to meet up the clients. I thought he was coming back later, but then I realized he said he couldn't, so I had to take the clients to dinner," he tried to add confidence to his voice but failed miserably as Bharti was in no mood to listen to any more lies.

She raised an eyebrow. "But you just said you were with Manoj. You never spoke about any clients. The meeting was between you and Manoj and not the clients. You had said you are going to work on some production schedule of the next campaign. So don't try to fool me into your stories. I have had enough of this shit."

"Yes, I said I was with Manoj. That was because I knew you wouldn't understand. It's complicated to manage this large business and it's very difficult to explain each and everything to you. You know nothing about managing a business," he said insultingly.

"Oh yes, you are right. I do not understand your business which runs in losses, the money doesn't come home, but the clients keep increasing. Yes, I do not understand this sort of business. In fact, I don't understand a word of what you are saying."

"You're so unreasonable, Bharti." His voice was becoming louder.

"Oh, all right, now I am unreasonable because I am asking you questions for the first time in my life? Is that your problem? You know in your heart that you are wrong. And that is all that matters! Fine, I will let it go and believe you, if that will stop this argument," she said despairingly.

Their thoughts were on disconnected zones. Neither of them really wanted to get mixed up in long discussions about who had been where, as it was treacherous ground and they could both end up getting found out.

He broke the silence. "Let's not fight like teenagers. I would like to make it up to you and take you out for a nice dinner tomorrow."

She was noncommittal. "Shirish Roy had called in and invited us to join him for a party at his place tomorrow. That's the reason I called you back. But I am not sure if I want to go there anymore."

"Maybe we can go there tomorrow. He is known to throw great parties," Sanjay said.

"I suppose so." She turned out the light on her side of the bed and lay with her back toward him.

He lit a cigarette. "I'm not tired," he remarked.

"Why don't you watch a movie? You bought in a few DVDs which are piled away on the side table. Whenever I clean the room and keep them away, you fight with me and keep them back on the table."

Sanjay weighed the question for a moment.

"I am not sure if I want to watch a movie."

"I need to sleep, so please switch off the light." Bharti wanted this ordeal to end. Her head was aching with this argument.

"That's a pretty nightdress. Is it new?"

"No, it's pretty old and I have worn it umpteen times." She sighed tolerantly, wishing he would go to sleep and let her sleep too.

He leaned over and kissed her on the cheek. She moved away promptly as if an insect had bitten her. She was shocked at Sanjay's action. After all those nights she had laid here waiting for him, he chose to make love tonight! *What does he think of himself? Am I his slave? Has he married me so that I manage his house? Go out to parties with him to keep up his good image? Keep lying with my legs open so that someday he may decide to make love to me!*

Sanjay launched himself across the bed before Bharti moved so much as another muscle. A wall of hard muscle flattened her breasts before his hands manacled her wrists and held her away so they no longer touched. Sanjay's arms came around her, clutching her tightly. He loosened his robe and lifted her night dress up to the knees. There was hurriedness in his act, as if he just wanted to get done with it. He slid down her panty with his right foot as he thrust his weight on her.

A vein throbbed at his temple. His hands clenched and unclenched. Sanjay stared at her for a long drawn-out moment.

"Lift your leg for me," he said.

As she followed his whispered instructions, he propped himself up on his elbows, then swung his legs over the edge of the bed and entered her as she reluctantly made way for him by spreading her legs. He nuzzled at her neck and pinched her nipples again. Hard. The ache shot through her, coinciding with his rocking motion. Pain coalesced into intense rapture. Sanjay quickened his rocking, stroking against her body. He clutched her, with hips still pumping, his head thrown back and face screwed up in an expression of agony. It surprised Bharti to know that he had no expression of pleasure on his face, just like her. She was surprised that she had waited countless nights for this moment and when this moment had come, she wasn't feeling good about it. She wanted pure love from Sanjay, but now that she knew he was lying to her, she just could not enjoy the physical act.

Bharti bit her lip, trying to contain the building whimper of pain and frustration. She lay there, rimming her dry lips with her tongue, considering for one burdened moment whether she really had to go through this. *I wish I could put an end to this situation. I wish I could make Sanjay realize what an ass he is. For once, only for once!*

He rode her firmly, with a controlled greed that was completely intolerable. He pushed deeper and settled his body tightly over hers and she felt the weight of his body on hers. He wanted nothing from her, just the mindless eruption of his pleasure as he moved mechanically inside her. Nothing for her, but she felt him pulsing, poking, almost as if he just badly needed a release.

She made a soughing sound. She couldn't move; he was mounted on her, jammed so tightly against her, so deeply within her. She could barely breathe, and every organ cried out in pain. She wished she could make Sanjay pay for what he had done to her. She wished she could give him the lonely nights she had lived for so long. She wished this was over.

He went into her quick and hard. He undulated and poled still deeper, as he lifted her more tightly into the cradle of his hips and pushed inside with short tight strokes. She was helpless; she was enveloped by him, utterly controlled by him and she hated it. Every second of it, every stroke, his fake possession, his lack of lust for her, and his authority subjugating her strength. She sunk in the thick pillow to hide her hatred as he kept moving inside her. He plunged into her again and she girded herself to fake it, to make him feel that she was with him now. Then there was that long lush silence in the aftermath of his release.

She wanted to feel loved. But she felt used. She wondered how love had vanished from their relationship.

Afterward, he collapsed on top of her. But she wished he'd get off of her, that he was far away from her. He was heavy, sweaty with his exertions, and she didn't like how he had used her tonight.

"That was spectacular," he said. "Hope it was good for you too."

She faked her pleasure. She nodded and said, "It was."

He switched off the lights. "Good night. Sweet dreams."

She forced her eyes shut to lock in the tears. "Good night."

He lay there and thought about how hot Trisha was.

She lay there and thought about how benevolent and responsive Ankit was.

At last they both fell asleep to their own sweet dreams, where they believed they had found love.

Abhinav Deo called up Trisha to cancel his rendezvous. While he had planned to spend the night with her, he got a better treat.

"Why are you cancelling the plan? What's the issue? Don't you like me?" asked Trisha.

"What's not to fancy?" Abhinav threw up his hands, wondering how to say no to this girl.

"So you do fancy me, but you won't see me."

"Listen, baby, I'm all tied up tonight. A friend of mine has referred to me a young girl who wants to become a star. My friend has highly recommended her." He looked at the naked girl on his bed and smiled.

"Oh." Trisha said playfully. "Look, I'm very flexible. I don't believe in the saying that two's a company and three's a crowd!"

"Do you mean what I think you mean?" he questioned as he turned around to the girl sitting on his bed, his eyes lighting up in anticipation. "Are you sure?"

"Of course I do." She purred. "You have a good taste because you chose me. So I am sure that your companion will be a good one. I don't mind experimenting a bit unless she has a problem with that."

"Just hold on a minute, let me check." Abhinav said, and the phone was muffled. He talked to the other girl and explained the threesome plan. To his surprise, she just smiled to the suggestion.

He understood that either she was completely a slut or really desperate to be a movie star. Or both.

Trisha waited patiently, and soon his voice came back full of interest. "Come soon. We'll be waiting for you."

She hung up, smiling, and made her way leisurely to her dressing table, where for the next twenty minutes she touched up her makeup and rearranged her hair so that it fell around her shoulders thick and shiny. She looked very beautiful, young, sexy and attractive. Her figure was shown off to its best advantage in the low-cut pink dress she was wearing.

She hailed a taxi and directed it to Abhinav Deo's place. She was fed up with Sanjay Kapoor. Stupid ass! Just who did he think he was? At first their affair had been fun. She enjoyed affairs with rich married men; they were a class apart, and usually happy to have a no strings affair. But Sanjay had started getting obsessed. Also, she had erroneously thought he might be able to help her in her career. She thought Sanjay had done absolutely nothing for her. Being the model for the Lasense television commercial appeared to lead to a dead end. Now she could get to Abhinav Deo instead.

The taxi pulled up at Abhinav Deo's house. She looked at his house surrounded by a lush green garden. The house was huge, straight off the pages of a novel. She stepped out of the taxi and walked onto the driveway.

There were fountains everywhere, surrounded by flowers of all colours and sizes. Their scents filled the air. With a contented smile, she looked around at all the unusual colours. The trees and grass were appearing more turquoise than green in the overhead lights. The flowers had colours so bright and vivid, they appeared almost neon.

She wished she could live in such a big house too which had flower-lined streets and a large balcony to admire nature. Life would be great in a house like this, she thought.

She rang the doorbell. Almost instantly, a doorman appeared. "May I help you?"

"My name is Trisha Mehra. Abhinav is expecting me." She glanced inside. It was like a castle inside the entryway, with a thick, plush carpet, stone walls where an ornate wall-sized painting hung above a decorated table, an antique chandelier shed soft subtle light, and another ornate door was set opposite the entrance.

"Oh sure! This way, please."

He motioned her into a marble-floored living room. A luxurious leather sofa set was comfortably situated around it, an expensive rug on the floor, and tables along the walls on either side, with crystal vases full of fresh flowers and lovely gilded paintings above them. She didn't know what she expected, but it wasn't this haute hushed elegance, this interior design marvel layout of the perfect living room done in earth tones and off-whites, sparkling crystal, and accents of brass and burgundy.

"Go to the first floor." He motioned her towards the staircase which led to Abhinav's room.

No backing down now. She stepped in on the first stair tentatively and then rushed across the others and pushed into the first door that she came across.

"Where have you been? We both have been waiting for you," Abhinav demanded.

She smiled apologetically, walked into his room and sat down, crossing her legs carefully to be sure there was the maximum amount of thigh showing. She knew she looked great.

"I'm so sorry, I got a bit late." she said. "But let me make up for it."

She kissed him, swooping over his body and into his mouth, her demanding tongue softening against his as she found his willing; as he melted into the kiss, into her tongue. She was a good kisser, just enough wet and heat to make his body twinge with need.

"I didn't know," he murmured against her lips, "when I talked to you over phone that you would be interested in…"

"You would know everything tonight," she whispered and took his tongue in a long, lingering kiss.

He clearly loved to kiss and probably had kissed many women just like that. But she didn't care.

"Let me melt in your mouth," she kissed him with an expertise that caught him by surprise. The way she licked him and then slowly insinuated her tongue between his lips; her kiss was wonderful, so fragile in its demand of him.

She claimed his mouth again, he stroked her smooth thighs, ran his hand all the way down her leg to her toes, slid his hand upward to the hem of her dress and pulled it up over her hips to find what he knew he would find; that she was naked beneath her dress and her body was hot for him.

She kissed him, but he immediately took over, his lips settling hard and sensuously on hers as he delved into her mouth with sensuous movements of his tongue. She took him to some other plane, a place where only sensation existed. All he could do was hang on and let her do what she wanted to do. His mouth devoured her, taking her pleasure deep into himself, not letting her pull away, back away. He couldn't move, could hardly breathe or respond to her kisses.

"Hope you accept the apology."

"Definitely. That's a good start. Phew!" he exclaimed. "Why don't you join my friend in the other room? She is waiting for you. I have told her that a hot girl named Trisha is here to spend the evening with us." Abhinav grinned.

"Huh, in that case do tell me her name. I should at least know who I am sleeping with," Trisha replied with coolness. She had never done a threesome before but she knew it was every guy's fantasy. She wanted Abhinav to be happy so that he helped her in return.

"Her name is Reena. But mind you, she is too hot to handle."

"Too hot to handle, let's see!"

"Try not to burn yourself up. I want you girls to start while I watch the live show."

Trisha looked puzzled. "You are not going to join?"

"I will, what's the rush?" He chuckled.

With a devilish grin, Trisha walked over to the other room. She looked down on Reena and gave her a warm smile while Abhinav stood at the side and watched. Reena's sleepy face had a look of complete satisfaction. As if she had just enjoyed a great climax or a great sleep. Trisha lovingly ran her fingers across Reena's exposed leg. She brushed her skin from ankle to thigh, gently circling what she knew to be a girl's sensitive areas. Reena moaned and turned onto her back, trying to get away from the touch. The movement exposed more of her naked body. Trisha gazed at her, she couldn't help but feel a little jealous of Reena's breasts. She had a pair a bit better than hers. But she knew she had better legs so she quickly brushed her jealousy aside.

Trisha leaned down and flicked one of Reena's exposed nipples with her tongue. Excited, she advanced from flicking and engulfed the nipple, sucking in her breast. Waking up, Reena realized it was the girl Abhinav had mentioned. Reena gave her a smile.

"Well, you are a gorgeous piece, too," she said, stroking the side of Trisha's face.

Trisha's eyes widened a little and then turned back toward the woman who grinned at them. "Come here," Trisha said, pulling Reena's face up to meet hers. She kissed her gently on the lips. As they made contact, Reena opened her mouth. Trisha took the invitation and slipped her tongue in. Their tongues danced against each other, swirling and batting.

Trisha's heartbeat quickened with pleasure. She pulled Reena in tighter and moved her free hand down to one of her bare breasts. She caressed her breasts, eliciting a moan. Reena pawed her as well. She grabbed the hemline of Trisha's dress and tried to pull it up.

Feeling what she was doing, Trisha broke away from the kiss and stood up from the bed. She grabbed the bottom of her dress and pulled it off, leaving her only in her pink bra. Still in bed, Reena pulled back the covers, fully exposing her naked flesh to her new friend. Neither of them wanted to deny each other.

Reena smiled at her. Slowly, Reena ran her hands across Trisha's body, from her breasts to her hips, fingers tracing under the waist. She reached up and undid the clasp holding her bra closed, popping the garment free. She tossed it aside and cupped her small breasts, teasing her nipples. Reena gently stroked her as Abhinav watched. The light from the chandelier played against Trisha's skin, enhancing her soft beauty.

Trisha stood there completely nude. Her body cried with need for a man, but Abhinav just stood in the corner. She had never done it with a girl, but she was enjoying every bit of it. So she thought she should go on with it. She climbed into bed with Reena. They held each other close, making as much contact as they could. Their mouths met again and danced with each other. Slowly, she dragged her wet, soft tongue across Reena's lips. Her touch was gentle and loving. She moved her tongue from her lips to her cleavage to her belly button. She took circles around the belly button for a while before moving down to the valley of lust.

Reena moaned in appreciation. "God, that feels good. Next time I need to get high, I'll be sure to give you a call," she said.

"You do that," Trisha said, lifting her head from between Reena's legs.

Reena nodded as Trisha slowly slid her hand between her legs. The second her soft palm cupped her, she cried out, bucking her hips against Trisha's hand. Wetness coated the inside of her thighs, making her slick and ready. Trisha moaned and dragged her finger along her entrance with maddening skill. Reena's knees almost buckled and if not for Trisha's other arm around her ribs, she would have fallen flat. Every part of her was on fire as Trisha moved her lips to lick at her breasts, her other hand continued to move in and out, making Reena go crazy. Together they played with each other, and drove mad with need.

Reena pushed two fingers deep inside Trisha to return the favour. She moaned, thrusting her hips forward to take her deeper. Her body clenched at the invasion, wanting more, wanting it harder.

"Oh I like this!" Trisha sighed as they continued the teasing movements.

Trisha stopped and made Reena lie down on the bed. She climbed on her in a motion so slow that it gave goose bumps to Reena. Trisha faced Reena's legs and moved her lips to lick her entrance. She had always wanted to try the-sixty-nine-position with a girl. Reena panted, desperate now for the feel of Trisha's mouth on her aching mound. Trisha's breath was hot and harsh as she leaned forward, flicking her tongue out to circle her vertical lips. Trisha's tongue plunged deep into her and she shuddered, holding fast to her hips.

Trisha stopped and looked back at Reena, eyeing her to return the favour. Reena followed her and lifted her face by holding Trisha's thighs as support. Reena's rough breathing vibrated against her back as she too plunged her tongue into Trisha's entrance. Trisha moaned. "Like that, baby?" Reena murmured from under her and she nodded, completely beyond any speech.

Trisha jerked, startled by the sudden full, flaming sensation. Reena kept licking at her while Trisha plunged her tongue deeper into her. They moved together as one, and the dual sensation of them licking each other had them hanging dangerously on the edge of release. They'd never felt anything so wild, so erotic and they wanted more.

"Oh god! It feels…" Trisha groaned as they changed their strategy, this time thrusting opposite each other, and the constant brushing of the thin wall that separated their passages sent fiery pleasure inside. Trisha panted, desperate for air as her body convulsed, tightening her walls around Reena's tongue. Reena moaned and increased the pressure of her tongue putting more pressure on her sensitive spot that Trisha never knew existed. With a howling yelp, her body tensed, then exploded into a million tiny pieces.

The two women sucked and moaned. Sweat beaded on both. The air filled with the sounds and smells of raw, passionate sex.

Abhinav was amazed at the sexy sight in front of him. He never would've thought that he'd find his latest conquest naked and in bed with another naked woman who was busy eating her out. *This is my lucky day,* he thought. His manhood turned to steel, tenting the robe further away from his body.

Reena stroked Trisha's hair and pulled her up, pushing her towards Abhinav. "Meet the man that almost broke me a few hours ago," she said.

Trisha looked over Abhinav with hungry eyes. They giggled as they turned to attack Abhinav. He laughed and raised the whiskey to his lips as they stripped him of his robe. Tumbling onto the piles of clothing, Abhinav pulled them down with him, his mouth suckling eager breasts, hands seeking, stroking, tugging and caressing. Soon the giggles turned to moans.

Abhinav paid attention to Trisha's breasts and she liked it. Her face twisted and she gasped. His hand slid down Reena's stomach into her fluffy mound of springy curls. Trisha was close enough to see his fingers pressing right into Reena's body and hear the sounds of pleasure she made. Trisha watched, unable to look away, as his manhood grew to proportions beyond belief.

"Come on girls, don't make me do all the work," he growled softly, tugging on one breast with one hand and moving the other hand on the other girl.

"Oh Abhinav…" Reena groaned.

"Mmm, Abhinav…" Trisha moaned.

The voices flowed across the space between Trisha and the writhing twosome and touched something deep inside her. Her own nipples were hard and aching and she could feel her getting wet against her heated flesh. She tried to hold back a squirm as Reena moved down on her and kissed her. She gasped as Reena started touching her lips on her. Reena groaned and writhed as Abhinav moved his hand in a continuous rhythm against her sensitive valley. Trisha echoed the rhythm and for one precious moment felt herself a part of the group; one of the naked, writhing, heaving bodies, experiencing the thrilling touch of flesh on flesh.

The air turned hot around them, the moans becoming grunts and gasps as they hunted their purpose.

Trisha wiggled her body seductively towards Abhinav. The openness in her eyes kicked out the foundation of his restraint and he did what he'd been wanting to do. He took her mouth, and a little taste only made him want more. He rolled his tongue over hers. She moulded herself to him as if she couldn't get close enough. The twitchy edgy need for two girls threatened to explode inside him. He slid his hands over Trisha's bottom, curling her into his hardness, and she automatically meshed with him, moving gracefully.

In her mouth, he tasted her struggle, the barest hint of hesitation and wild voluptuous desire. Filled with an overwhelming urge to possess her, he wanted to make the slight hesitation disappear. He wanted to be inside Trisha. He wanted to be inside Reena too. Maybe then his gnawing need would be eased.

He slipped his hands to touch Trisha's thighs and rubbed his mouth over the softness of her neck. "Abhinav…" Trisha whispered in a breathless voice of both hesitation and invitation.

He took it as an invitation and stepped up behind her and drove himself in.

"Aah!" she cried at his massive intrusion. "Abhinav," she said. "This is crazy."

"It is. Do you want me to stop?" he asked, caressing the tender spot.

Trisha gasped and closed her eyes. "No."

Abhinav grabbed her hips and began to move faster. Now that he was deep inside, he wasn't going to stop until he emptied himself. Abhinav pulled her hair, twisting her head around so she could see him ride her. Abhinav grabbed her hips again and adjusted his angle. He placed both feet on the bed and squatted above her, truly mounting her.

Trisha screamed at the new angle. "Oh God, that's it, right there. Don't stop! Please don't stop." She started to moan from the passion playing with all her senses. Reena gently pulled Trisha's head to her breasts, comforting her. She watched Trisha's face contort and twist with pleasure. With her eyes closed and mouth agape, Reena had never seen a sight like this. She felt her body start to moisten again and kissed Trisha deeply and lovingly.

Seeing the two girls kiss each other drove Abhinav wild. He pulled out from Trisha. "Turn over," he commanded her.

The two girls snapped out of their revelry and looked at him confused.

"I said turn over."

Trisha slowly pushed herself off Reena and flopped down onto her back. She opened her legs, welcoming him back in. Abhinav pounced and threw her left leg over his shoulder. The right he placed around his waist. He slowly inserted himself back in. He wanted to enjoy the show.

Trisha whimpered as he pushed himself back in. The sudden change in pace caught her off guard. Now he moved slowly to allow Reena to intervene the process.

Reena watched for a second before laying herself onto Trisha. She lowered her head down to where it mattered most and slithered her tongue making Trisha go crazy because of the simultaneous licking and thumping. Trisha let out a high-pitched moan and pulled her legs and arms tighter around her lovers. "Ooooooh," she cried. "This is too much. I can't handle this." She dialled in Sanjay so that he could hear her moans. So that he could imagine how much fun she was having. She wanted him to know that she was not his slave.

"Don't worry, baby," Reena said. "I'll take care of you." She bowed her head again and resumed the licking. As Reena bent down to lick Trisha, she realized that Trisha had decided to return the favour. Trisha licked beneath Reena, making it hard for her to concentrate.

Reena felt Trisha's body start to tremble. She moved back and kissed Abhinav, as he shuddered to a climax along with Trisha. Trisha woke up from her orgasm and lay there too exhausted to move. She gaped at him in surprise. She would never have dreamed she would do such a thing. The silence in the room might as well have been as deafening as the thunder rolling inside her.

Trisha stared at herself in the dressing room mirror. Abhinav's partner Shirish had organized the biggest party of the town and she was dressing up for that.

Pursing her lips, Trisha contemplated her reflection. The blue of the outfit really brought out her eyes, but it was so different from what she usually wore. The pants were silk, loose at the waist and tapered at the ankle. The top had long sleeves that flared out above the wrist. It had straps that wrapped around and tied in a knot just below her rib cage, showing off a good portion of her flat stomach.

Abhinav looked at her. A bit worried.

"The party is at the Hilton Hotel. What happened to you? Usually I see you in designer dresses and today you are wearing pants and a top?

"I thought it's a party where elegant upper class people would be coming. So I have tried to dress up a bit classy, you see."

"You are right. But still, your pants and top aren't dressy enough. It's going to be the biggest party of the town. You need to look really appealing as you are going to be by my side," Abhinav said. "Why don't you try some dress from my closet? I always have a few dresses lined up in my closet to make sure my date looks as hot as I want her to look." He replied with a radiant smile on his face.

Trisha realized that the wardrobe had far too sophisticated clothes than what she was wearing.

Reaching into a closet at the back of his room, he pulled out a dress and held it up for her to see. "What do you think of this? I'll bet it will look much better on you and will be easier for me to take off." Abhinav chuckled.

She gasped softly. A royal blue silk dress – soft and delicate. Superbly cut, it had a high choke neck in front, but the back was totally bare, from shoulder to shoulder and from neck to waist.

Involuntarily, she reached out to touch it. "Oh," she said softly.

"Here. Put it on."

She looked up into his eyes and then her chin lifted rebelliously as she backed away. "I look awesome in this thing," she reminded him.

He sighed. "I am not saying that you are not looking good, but you'll look out of this world in this thing and you know why it is required today." His mouth twisted cynically.

"You don't think it's too…"

"Too what?"

"Slutty?"

"Slutty? As if you care about that! You will look really tempting in this dress." Abhinav grinned at her through the mirror. "Everyone will drool over when they see you in this. You need to make a good impression tonight."

Trisha looked convinced as she moved her fingers on the expensive dress.

"Get dressed, Trisha," he said quietly, touching her cheek with his forefinger, setting off a trail of sensation. "We're late. And I plan to make quite an entrance."

The Jinxx was a swanky private club and Trisha was very glad she'd worn the blue silk dress caressing her thighs much above her knees. She assumed it must belong to one of Abhinav's many rumoured play girls. It was not the first time she had tried on clothes from someone else's wardrobe, but it was the first time she had filled out the seams just perfect. He had been right; it fit like a glove. And when she'd seen the look in his eyes as she came out of the room all ready to go, she'd felt the kind of thrill she used to get as a child at the fair when the roller coaster went into a sudden dive.

Trisha was just a little nervous. She hesitated just outside the entrance.

A small orchestra was playing a waltz against the background of the clinking of expensive crystal mixed with light conversation. Trisha shook her head. The party was sounding upper class.

"Ready?" he asked, folding her hand into the crook of his arm.

She looked up into his eyes and furrowed her nose. "I don't know," she said impishly.

He laughed softly and she felt fear spreading deep inside her.

They swept into a large hall. For a moment, Trisha was blinded by the flash from the chandeliers, but as her vision cleared, she realized they were strolling into a small crowd standing in front of a tall man with iron gray hair and proud eyes.

"Shirish," Abhinav said. "I'd like you to meet someone very special. This is Trisha Mehra. She has graciously consented to work in our next movie."

Shirish had to be shocked by the news, but he didn't let it show.

'Well, Abhinav," he said softly. "You should have told me. Isn't this the Lasense girl? I think I saw her at the launch party. Sanjay's wife Bharti told me that you had already finalized her, but I didn't believe her at that point of time."

"I wanted it to be a surprise," he told Shirish smoothly.

"Oh, I'm surprised," Shirish said, fixing him with a steely glare. "Surprised and utterly unconvinced."

Trisha noted the look between the two of them and instinct told her she was being thrust into an argument that had been going on long before she arrived. But there was no time for analysis, as Abhinav was taking her into his arms as he saw Sanjay entering the party.

Shirish stepped towards the main gate and welcomed him.

"Have you decided not to bring Bharti to this party? Where is she?" asked Shirish, a look of concern in his eyes.

"Oh no, it's not like that. Bharti wasn't feeling too well so she decided to meet a doctor. If she feels better, she will try and come," replied Sanjay with a forced smile on his face. He was happy that Bharti had decided not to come. At least that would give him some time with Trisha.

They walked towards the bar and Sanjay ordered a large scotch on the rocks and they started gossiping. Couple of drinks later, Shirish was pulled by a few guests and Sanjay was left alone. He asked the bartender to make a stiff peg for him. He was missing Trisha and hoped that the alcohol could fill the hollowness inside him. His eyes ached for Trisha.

Sanjay looked around and froze when he saw Trisha standing close to Abhinav Deo. He was already furious by her phone call in which he had heard her moaning and groaning with Abhinav. Their togetherness fuelled up the fire in him. He ordered for another large drink and gulped it down in one go. The liquid burned inside, making him ache, but the pain was much lesser than what he could feel by seeing Trisha standing next to Abhinav.

Abhinav eyed the orchestra and they played his favourite songs. Abhinav and Trisha danced closely. Sanjay got really jealous of their togetherness and gulped down a few more drinks. The bartender made generous pegs for him and he honoured the pegs with a swift bottoms up.

After the dance, Trisha left Abhinav as he had to meet a lot of guests and walked around the party. Her eyes searched for Sanjay.

She found him standing alone near the second bar close to the staircase. He seemed to be pretty drunk and wasted. She also saw the bitterness, but noted the sad bewilderment of a lover who saw the ones he loved best slipping from him in some deep, emotional way. She felt bad for him. For some inexplicable reason, Trisha's heart for a moment went out to Sanjay.

She walked behind Sanjay and edged quietly up behind him. Pressing her body against his back, she covered his eyes with her hands and said, "Guess who, baby?"

There was no mistaking that body. He was astonished but sharply excited. She had the most incredible effect on him: he just had to know she was there to want her. He turned slowly, eyes looking around to see if anyone was observing them.

"Hello, Trisha."

"Hello, Trisha." She mimicked his voice. "Don't I get a better welcome than that darling? I just wanted to say that I was really missing you."

She eyed the bartender and he repeated Sanjay's drink. Sanjay held the glass in his hand and stepped unsteadily towards Trisha. "Really? It looks like you are having a ball with Abhinav."

"That's the problem sweetheart. You just believe what you see."

"What else do you want me to believe?"

"You need to look beyond what all the people in the party can see. I am with Abhinav because I want to get a role in the movie. That's it. It's a business transaction and once it's over, I am all yours."

"I don't understand you Trisha!" He gulped down his drink and slammed the glass on the bar. "You are sleeping with that rascal Abhinav and you are saying it's a business deal? How is that possible?"

Trisha eyed the bartender and he again made a stiff peg for Sanjay and handed it over to him.

"Sweetheart, that's the point. He makes me a star and in exchange I give my body to him. It's simple." Trisha replied with a straight face. "What you need to believe is that he can have my body, but not my soul."

Sanjay gulped down his drink and stepped forward to hug her. When his arms held her, he realized that she was wearing a backless dress. He snaked his arms around her waist and felt the warmth of her body. With soft feminine curves, Trisha was enough to make him forget his own name. She blew out a breath, making her long bangs flutter over his hands, and he wondered if she knew how sexy that was. God, the woman was perfection on high heels. Tall and slender, she had curves in all his favourite places. He'd always had a thing for her.

Sanjay knew this road was crazy and impulsive, not to mention reckless, but the warmth of her body made his manhood harden in new and painful proportions inside his pants. Man, she was killing him there. Before he could say anything, she reached out and pulled his head back from the embrace. He could have stopped her, probably should have, but with an invitation like the one he was getting, what was a man supposed to do?

"Hey baby, why don't we go find a quiet corner somewhere? We need to clear some things out. I promised you the fantasy of making out secretly in a public event. What can be a better opportunity than this?" She could smell the lingering scent of alcohol that seemed to ooze from his every pore.

Considering they were in the middle of the party where anyone could see them, being close to her was a little careless. But it also fulfilled a long-time fantasy – part of it anyway – and he wasn't about to pass up the chance to grab it, or her, with both hands.

"I want you," she whispered against his mouth.

He lifted his head with a groan. "I want you, too. But where do we go?"

"I think we can find some private corner upstairs?"

He gazed down at her, his dark eyes smouldering. He muttered something under his breath, which she didn't catch. She pressed a kiss to his cheek, then turned and started for the stairs only to stop and look at him. "Come, let's fulfil our fantasy that we had to leave unfinished in the green room that day."

His heart almost skipped a beat and he followed her to the first floor. "Hurry up," Trisha called him. Then he hurried up the remaining steps unsteadily due to the excessive alcohol flowing in his body.

Abhinav stepped out from behind a pillar next to the staircase, took out his mobile and dialled Bharti's number. "Hi Bharti. I need to tell you something about your husband."

"Hi. Do I know you? What nonsense is this?" she replied coldly planning to disconnect the call.

"Wait wait. It's me, Abhinav Deo."

"Abhinav? It's been so long. What happened?"

"If you disconnect the call today, you will never come to know what your husband is doing behind your back," he said swiftly.

Dumbstruck, Bharti just stood there wondering what she had just heard.

"You there?" Abhinav prodded after a moment of confusing silence.

"Where is he?"

"In Shirish Roy's house, on the terrace."

Bharti disconnected the call and rushed for the party.

Abhinav stepped forward and looked upstairs. Finally Trisha and Sanjay had reached the terrace. And fnally, he could get his revenge.

Sanjay and Trisha walked to a corner where no one could see or hear them, or so they thought.

She was leaning over the wall, the corners of her breasts peeking sideways from her dress. He swallowed hard. She undid the top button of his shirt. Her pulse skipped a beat. Grinning, she hastily undid the rest of the buttons on his shirt, then slipped her hands inside to get up close and personal with him. She caught her breath as he swooped forward to kiss her again. His mouth was firm and demanding on hers, his tongue plunging into her mouth to take complete and total possession of hers. She threaded her fingers into his dark hair, but he was already kissing his way along the curve of her jaw and down her neck. She dropped her head back, thrusting her breasts out in invitation.

"Right now, I am going to put up a fight with you, and I am sure you will like it. I know you like to force yourself upon me." She swallowed as his hand slid on her and cupped her breasts, squeezing them hard under the silky fabric of her dress.

"Do you want me to kiss you yet?" he hissed.

"No," she replied, continuing the game.

He pressed his thigh between her legs, putting mild but persistent pressure against her. "Do you want me here?"

"No, I don't want you at all," she snapped.

"Liar," he said, his lips thinning out into a malicious grin. "You are not putting up a real fight, Trisha. I want you to put up a real fight. Then it would be really ecstatic to force you into lovemaking."

He was over her, straddling her thighs beneath him. Grabbing her wrists as she tried to now really put up a real fight. He pinned them to the floor on either side of her head, effectively holding her in place.

"Let me up," she gritted through her teeth as she wiggled to get out from under him.

He looked around and then kissed her forcefully. "Did you miss me?" he whispered. He jumped from wanting to kiss her to wanting to strangle her all in the same breath.

"Leave me alone. I want nothing to do with you," she continued the game by yelling at him.

"I'm smashed, you know. You're a bitch, leaving me thirsty for you."

She tried to pull her wrists from his grasp, but he held firm, applying pressure to the bones. She bit down on her lip to hide the wince of pain.

"Not until you understand that you are just mine."

"Let go of me," she replied through her clenched teeth.

He nibbled at her ear, rubbing his body against her.

A heartbeat later, that wasn't close enough. Too many clothes separated their straining bodies. Sanjay slid his lips over Trisha's in an open-mouthed kiss that exploded on his senses, sucking him into the magical spell she cast. Time seemed to slow down. Each tiny gasp from Trisha made him go hard until all he could think of was plunging into her.

Sanjay gasped at the streak of pleasure and power over her. He was drunk and cold and her hot body warmed him, seduced him, and he gave into the temptation, exploring, gliding his hands over her smooth muscles as she played the role of a girl being forced into sex.

Her breasts strained against the satin dress and he was eager to touch them. She expected him to take off his dress, but instead, he just pulled the dress up forcefully. The dress was too silky and delicate and it ripped apart, freeing her breasts from their confines. He hungrily bent down to take one of her nipples in his mouth and sucked on it. His mouth was warm, his tongue like a razor as it teased and tormented her, and she moaned as he turned his attention to the other breast to do the same thing. While he paid attention to that nipple, he took the other between his thumb and forefinger and rolled it back and forth. It was enough to drive her crazy, and yet she murmured a protest.

Sanjay shivered with the desire tingling through his body. Blood rushed to places that had no business paying attention to Trisha's proximity. She was his. And that was all that mattered.

Sanjay wanted a whole lot of things at once. He wanted to take her with his hands and mouth and body. He wanted to be inside her. Slow down, he told himself, sucking in a deep breath of air. But he couldn't. She gasped, digging her fingers into his biceps. "What are—"

With each helpless movement of her body, he grew harder and needier. The taste and sound of her was so addictive, he didn't want to stop.

"Stop!" she finally begged in a muffled voice from under his palm.

"I can't—"

She shook her head helplessly.

"I want—"

Sanjay's dark eyes asked for everything his words couldn't. Sanjay was consumed with the primitive need to make her his. She didn't have time to react before he skimmed one of his hands up her thighs. His fingers slid into her secret, damp swollen place, and he groaned. "I want you, Trisha."

"Damn you," she snarled.

"Shut up," he commanded.

He still had her hands trapped above her head, and she struggled against his hold, but he wouldn't let her go. His eyes lit with dark fire, and he took her mouth and took her body. He unbuckled his trousers with his left hand as he almost bit her mouth, neck and breasts. He dipped his head, hungrily sucking at her nipple. She cried out, arching her back and grinding her hips. Trisha's tormented groan throbbed in the air between them.

"You are mine."

Sanjay leaned over her body, his chest brushing her sensitive nipples. She felt his erection brushing the entrance to her body. Her body trembled. He shifted, spreading her thighs with his. He pressed forward, and she could feel the evidence of his hard arousal against her. Sanjay grinned up at her, apparently enjoying her nervousness. Then he parted her legs.

"Trisha." Her name came out on a sigh as he thrust inside her. He felt impossibly big inside her, larger than he had ever felt before. Making out in a public place forcefully had given him that excitement, he thought. He lowered his head and sucked on one taut nipple.

Trisha felt the dig of his teeth on the slope of her breast. Sanjay soared on top of her.

He thrust inside her, and Trisha could do nothing. Actually she could, but she didn't want to.

He pulled almost out, and then thrust back in hard.

"You are such a wild beast," she groaned, undulating beneath him.

She dropped her head against the cold floor, closed her eyes, and screamed as every part of her shattered. "You can't have me," she whispered, determined to put up a good fake fight to the very end.

"Look at me," he commanded.

She opened her eyes, staring into his eyes as his body rode out wave after wave. He kept pumping against her, prolonging his release until she thought she'd beg him to stop. With a low, deep growl, he pumped one final time. Pulling out of her, he let her fall completely to the cold floor. Sanjay held her tight as he rode the storm until the lightning and thunder calmed.

Trisha came to herself slowly, feeling Sanjay's heart thudding against her breasts. Her eyes flickered open even though she didn't remember closing them. Her hands felt across the floor. A slow smile curled across his handsome face. "I enjoyed the game, how about you?"

She put her mouth to his ears and said. "The game has just started."

When Bharti reached Shirish's house, Abhinav quickly guided her to the terrace. Once there, what she saw made her shout at the top of her voice. "What the hell are you doing Sanjay?"

Hearing the commotion, a few other people came rushing upstairs and stood behind Bharti to enjoy the show.

Sanjay was shocked to see all the people surrounding him.

Suddenly, Abhinav grabbed Sanjay by his hair, jerked his head back and punched him in the face. Gasping at the pain, he closed his eyes, then immediately released Trisha's wrist, allowing her to step back out of his reach.

"I think you have had enough fun for one night." Abhinav sneered as he again punched Sanjay on his face.

Trisha came running to Abhinav. "Thank God, you are here. This beast tried to rape me!"

Sanjay was shocked at the accusation. He had played this game many times with Trisha, but the outcome was never this dramatic.

"Are you all right?" Putting his finger under her chin, Abhinav tried to make her look at him as he covered her with his jacket.

Trisha broke down into fake tears.

"Security, come up here at once!" yelled Abhinav.

Shocked and sickened, Bharti backed away as she saw security guards running towards Sanjay.

"Bharti, Bharti! Just listen to me! It's not what it seems to be." Sanjay walked towards her, buckling his belt.

The security guards came up and surrounded him as he tried to push through them.

Dazed, Bharti ran back to the ground floor.

She was heading for the door when Shirish appeared and grabbed her arm. "What's the matter? You look terrible, what happened?"

She looked at him with unseeing eyes. "I've got to get out of here," she mumbled, pushing his arm away and making for the door.

Shirish caught hold of her arm again firmly. "Tell me what happened." He took her hand and held it tight. "Tell me, please," he repeated in a softer voice.

She looked at him with eyes full of shock. "I suspected that Sanjay flirted around with models maybe once in a while, but this is just some other level. Raping a girl in a party! I think he has lost his mind. It's horrible. Don't you know? Where the hell were you? Half of your guests are upstairs looking at the free show!"

"Oh God!" said Shirish. "That stupid son of a bitch! Look, I think the girl was drunk. Maybe he was trying to just get rid of her." Shirish tried to defend his friend.

Bharti's eyes were scornful. "I know what I saw, Shirish. Don't try to protect your friend."

"Shall I take you home?" Shirish asked.

She shook her head. "I can't do it anymore. This is it for me. I'm done with him and his infidelity. I want a divorce. I just hate him from the bottom of my heart." Her voice shook. "I don't ever want to see his face again. I hope he rots in hell."

"Look Bharti. It's not a good idea to take such harsh decisions while you're upset. Let me drop you home. I'll come straight back and talk to Sanjay and tell him not to go home tonight."

She laughed bitterly. "Not tonight? Please tell him not to come home ever again. Tell him to go to hell. Tell him to go and sleep with his slutty models. Tell him he can do whatever he wants. I'm through with him." She stepped out of the house as she saw a police car stopping in front of the house.

Policemen got out of the car and rushed towards the door. Shirish was surprised at the sudden arrival of the police.

"Can I help you, officer?" Shirish asked as the police looked eager to get inside.

"We've got information that there has been an attempted rape at this location. Please move out of the way and let the police do its job." He pushed his way inside and the team followed.

"Where is the crime scene?" The officer looked at a few people standing in the main hall.

Three to four people pointed their fingers upwards simultaneously, and the policemen ran one after the other towards the terrace. They looked around and saw a girl standing in torn clothes next to a guy, crying hysterically. The officer realized that she was the victim and went up to her. She had buried her head in Abhinav's shoulder.

"We need to know who did this to her," the officer asked Abhinav.

Before Abhinav could respond, Trisha turned around. "Officer, this is the man who tried to rape me." Trisha pointed towards Sanjay as she broke into sobs in Abhinav's arms.

Sanjay stood there motionless. He couldn't understand what was happening. He had made love to Trisha many times in the past. "That's not true, officer! This bitch is telling a lie. This is consensual sex and we have done this many times in the past." He blurted out in anger.

"You're under arrest on suspicion of rape." The officers walked towards Sanjay and surrounded him without listening to any of his explanations.

Sanjay's jaw dropped to the ground. "There must be some mistake. I am telling you this isn't rape. She is my lover and we have been together many times." He looked hopefully at Trisha.

"I have only worked in his agency for a television commercial. Other than that, I don't know what this man is saying," Trisha replied coldly.

Sanjay was zapped at her reply.

The police officers put a powerful hand on Sanjay and handcuffed him. He was escorted downstairs and everyone present in the party had their eyes on him. He could also hear a faint but persistent murmur of hushed voices, which was most likely his character assassination in progress.

The group stepped out of the house and walked across to the police van. Sanjay showed hesitation and tried to pull back from the van. The police team was in no mood to handle his tantrums and pushed him inside.

"This is outrageous. I want to call my lawyer," Sanjay shouted as the police forced him inside the jeep.

"Right now, you are under arrest for suspicion of rape. You will be given an opportunity to call your lawyer. And your lawyer better be good, because this is a crime with so many eye witnesses that even God can't save you," the officer replied.

The moment the police car sped away, lots of vans started pouring in with satellite dishes mounted on top of the vans. A large group of media journalists crowded the main entrance.

Abhinav, Trisha and other guests stood on the doorway, but the journalists wouldn't allow anyone to leave. They were swarming the entrance like bees. To manage the commotion, Abhinav raised a hand and requested everyone to be quiet. The journalists eyed each other and the noise subdued like the ending of a song in a systematic way.

Abhinav spoke again, "Dear friends, while we have always been cooperative in sharing all the news with you regarding our new movie releases, album launches, and other such stuff, this is something we don't want to talk about."

"We have got information that a renowned director has raped an aspiring model? Is that true?" An enthusiastic journalist shouted and others followed him as they pushed their microphones literally into Abhinav's mouth.

Abhinav looked at Trisha. He wasn't sure what to say or do. Trisha was still crying and had not recovered from the act. Before he could say anything, Trisha left his arm and walked a step ahead into the crowd.

"Coming forward is the hardest decision that I have made right now. Especially for a crime like rape where I know I am only going to lose everything that remains. But I have always been a fighter. And this is a fight I *want* to take up." Trisha wiped her tears. She was a clever bitch. She knew this would bring her to the front page of all newspapers. She really wanted this publicity.

The journalists and photographers snapped pictures of Trisha. Flashlights illuminated the dark night.

"Just because Sanjay Kapoor is rich and influential does not mean he can get away with rape. I am going to make sure he pays for his sins."

She stopped, looked back at Abhinav and eyed him to step forward.

"And I would also like to thank Abhinav Deo who saw what happened and had the courage to hit the bastard and stand by me." Abhinav stepped forward and made a solemn face as the flashlights blinded him.

"I would request you all to allow us to take Trisha home. She is devastated and needs to take rest," Abhinav spoke with a touch of concern in his voice.

The media journalists had got their scoop. They made way for her and the guests walked towards the parking lot. The drive to Abhinav's house was silent. Once there, Abhinav stepped out of his car and the driver then opened the door for Trisha. They walked together to his mansion which shone in the moonlight.

Trisha looked sad and troubled. Abhinav's jacket and his body next to her were keeping her warm. The driver gave the keys to Abhinav and walked away feeling sad for Trisha.

The moment they walked into the house, Trisha threw away the coat and started jumping up and down with a wicked laughter and Abhinav joined her.

"So? Do you now believe that I am good actor?" Trisha said.

"I had my doubts but…"

"But?"

"But now I am sure that you are a true actor. The way you made everyone believe that Sanjay had actually raped you was phenomenal. You executed the plan just the way we had planned it."

"Poor Sanjay, he is in the prison because of me." Trisha sighed.

"Well ,that was the plan and you did your role well. I wanted revenge and you wanted a role in the movie. It's definitely a win-win for both of us.

Abhinav walked toward Trisha and hugged her. "I think you played your part really well. Now the son of a bitch will rot in hell."

"Thank god Bharti came on time or we would have had to use Plan B. But I think it was more dramatic when it happened right in front of Bharti's eyes!" Trisha chirped.

"Where is the CD? Let me have a look at it. After all, it's my first movie!" Trisha grinned.

"He moved his hand inside his jacket and pulled out a CD."

"Good you suggested we record this," Abhinav said.

"And good that you told me where the surveillance cameras were, else I would have got fucked for no reason!"

"Well, I know every bit of Shirish's house and I am glad we have this backup with us," beamed Abhinav.

"We are a good team. I am impressed by the fact that you planned the party at Shirish's house where Sanjay had no clue of what he would land into."

"Yes, I didn't want Sanjay to get suspicious." Abhinav grinned. "Who wants a drink? I am going to grab one."

Walking behind the bar and pouring himself a peg of Scotch whisky, Abhinav turned around to look at Trisha. She stood sideways, with her shoulder leaning against the window. Her position allowed him just the right view, and he absolutely liked what he saw. Letting his gaze travel down the length of her, he admired her perfect figure, all the way from the tip of her lovable nose to the bottom of her well-rounded calves as he sipped his scotch.

His appraisal slowed at her firm, flat stomach and flawlessly rounded breasts. Blood that should have usually been used for thinking rapidly spread to areas south. *Damn.* Taking a deep breath, he tried to clear the not-so-decent thoughts that were running uncontrolled through his mind. Thoughts of making out with her were primary, and he groaned, trying to think of something else. They still had to execute the remaining part of the plan.

He realized he was stuck in a deep game of lust and there was no looking back.

"It's a victory," Trisha said.

"Definitely. But I am going to suck every penny out of him," replied Abhinav. "We have just executed the first part of the plan. Now I am going to send you to meet him in prison and ask him for the money as a settlement for taking back the rape charges or else he can rot in jail. He will have no choice but to sell the diamonds and hand us the money." Abhinav smiled at his vicious plan.

"That is my money! That bastard embezzled the money from my company," Abhinav continued.

"I will help you in the plan, but you need to remember your promise of making me a successful actress," replied Trisha.

"I will ensure you get what you deserve," he assured her.

"So what is the plan?" asked Trisha.

"I just told you the plan. What more do you want to know?" He gulped in his scotch.

"I need to have all the details of the plan," said Trisha.

"Ask me anything you want to," came the answer.

"How are we going to convince Sanjay to give you the money? He will put his best lawyers to use. We know that the rape case can be fought for years with no results."

"True, but we are not going to fight any case," Abhinav replied with a grin on his face.

"You are a slimy bastard, I must say," Trisha said with a naughty smile.

Abhinav beamed with pride at her comment. "Yes, what you are thinking is right. We are going to settle out of court."

Trisha kept the CD safely in her purse. "So I will go to the prison tomorrow and show the footage to Sanjay and threaten him that I will take this evidence to court."

"Yes, and that bastard will have no other choice but to pay you off!" said Abhinav in a decidedly stern tone.

Trisha smiled. "Your intellect just turns me on. It's great to be with a hot, intelligent and successful guy like you rather than being with Sanjay."

Abhinav beamed with arrogance. He turned around and walked back to Trisha. "It's done. I am eager to get the diamonds now."

"Don't you want to have something else first?" She looked him in the eyes and turned back towards the window.

Shaking his head, he tried to tell himself he didn't have time for this, no matter how appealing the package was. He had too much to do, too much at stake. Even as those thoughts went through his mind, he began to move towards her.

Stopping next to her, he leaned his shoulder against the window. She turned to look at him with eyes dazzling as emeralds. He could drown in those eyes. She turned to head back to the bar. He followed, watching the sway of her firm backside. That torn dress left absolutely nothing to the imagination, and his manhood twitched as he fought the desire to grab a handful of that ass, toss her onto the bar, and have his fill of her.

She scowled at him over her shoulder as though she knew what he was thinking, and he winked, incapable to resist teasing her. Just thinking about dipping his fingers into that tight bit of flesh set his blood on fire. Quietly, he walked up behind her and setting his glass on the counter, placed his hand along the side of her waist. He loved her figure. All the right curves in all the right places. His hand moved lower along her hip, and she stiffened. With a gasp, she turned around, craning her neck to look up at him.

She was so petite, barely reaching his shoulder. It made her seem fragile. But he knew fragile was the last thing this little spitfire was. He leaned forward, his hands resting against the bar on either side of her hips. Her breath fanned against his lips, and he inhaled the scent of alcohol. Her body tensed, but he ignored it and moved closer. So close, their noses almost touched. Her pulse throbbed in her neck, and he fought the urge to touch his lips to that spot, to soothe her fear and make her heart pound for a different reason.

"So what were you saying? What is it that you want me to have?" asked Abhinav.

"Unless I'm mistaken Abhinav, you forgot something," Trisha replied wickedly.

"Forgot what?" His voice sounded breathless, and she smiled inwardly.

His head dipped lower, and she shied away, bending backward over the bar.

"You forgot to say thank you."

She put her hand against his chest and pushed. He didn't budge. Well, parts of him bulged for sure. Her close proximity played mayhem with his senses as well as his manhood.

With an exasperated sigh, he scowled. "Fine. Thank you."

She bit back a grin. "Surely you can do better than that. How about a kiss?"

He closed his lips tightly to keep from laughing. He loved her unexpected remarks. He moved closer and rubbed the tip of his nose against hers. Her lips parted as she sucked in a quick breath. His finger trailed along the side of her throat. He felt a shiver run through her and lightly tapped her pulse point. He skimmed his fingers along her cheek. Her skin was smooth and soft beneath his fingertips. His gaze moved to her remarkable cleavage, and he noticed the quick rise and fall of her breasts. She was so beautiful, even now, his manhood twitched in his pants to have her, to feel her wet heat wrapping around him again.

Abhinav's breath brushed against her cheek, and she turned to find herself nose to nose with him. His eyes mirrored the tempest going on within her, and she swallowed nervously. His hungry gaze moved from her eyes to her lips, making her chest tighten. The evening had gone so well. Everything had happened as per plan. And the evening was about to get better.

Slowly, she lowered her head toward his, and he drew in a shaking breath. She rubbed her nose against the tip of his, the contact causing him to almost jump out of his skin. The electricity in that one simple touch sent tingles throughout his entire body. She continued to nibble and tease. Her patience and lack of urgency were erotic in themselves, and he opened his lips beneath her. She ran her tongue along his bottom lip before sliding it against his teeth, slowly exploring as if she had all the time in the world. Running her tongue along his teeth, she barely touched her tongue to his before retreating.

Trisha smiled. She had done her bit of seducing. Abhinav was turned on. He leaned closer. He wanted to taste more of her. Her flowery scent enveloped him, making him want to drown in it.

He cupped her face in his hands gently and deepened the kiss further. Wrapping her arms around his neck, she met his eager mouth with her own longing need. One kiss led to another and she couldn't seem to stop. Her body burned with fire, his fingers scorching every place he touched, and he touched everywhere.

"Abhinav," she sighed against his mouth. He could smell a male perfume on her, perhaps Sanjay's, but he was way beyond the point of return. Grabbing her at the waist, he pulled her onto his lap, her legs straddling his hips. Her knees rested on either side of him, causing her dress to ride up her thighs, exposing them. She didn't care.

Abhinav groaned and slanted his lips across hers. She was thrilled by the sound. She loved the fact that she had a strong effect on him. Reaching up, he removed her dress as his lips trailed a path down her neck. She sighed as his thumbs brushed across her hardened nipples through the lace of her bra. His fingers traced the edges of Trisha's bra before he slid it aside, freeing her breasts. He captured the hard peak in his mouth, his tongue stroking and teasing. Trisha buried her hands in his hair and tugged him closer, encouraging him to take more of her. With a gasp, she ground her aching valley against his hard manhood, the material of his trousers creating a friction that drove her wild.

Pulling at the buttons of his shirt, she opened it and slipped her hands inside, running her fingers along the smooth expanse of warm skin and hard muscle. She marvelled at his strength and smiled when she felt the muscles twitch beneath her exploring fingers.

He slid his palms up the outside of her thighs. She quivered at the feel of his fiery fingers against her skin. Abhinav murmured against her lips, "Feeling cold?"

"No," she said with a sigh.

He smiled a bit as he sucked her lower lip. "If you are, I can warm you up a bit." His hands cupped her bottom and brought her more firmly against his thick manhood. She groaned as his mouth consumed hers and his hands kneaded her behind, moving her in a slow rhythm against him that drove her wild.

Sliding one hand between their bodies, he let his fingers pursue the path along the top edge of her panties. Trisha held her breath as he moved lower and traced the edge along the inside of her thigh. His teeth nibbled her neck while he separated her vertical lips with his finger. He sucked on the spot where he could feel her pulse throbbing ever so gently.

Abhinav wanted to rip her panties off and lose himself in her, bury every inch of his aching manhood inside her, but he also didn't want it over yet. He was enjoying himself way too much. Bringing his mouth back to hers, his tongue traced her lips at the same time as his finger traced her entrance. He smiled as she arched against his hand, her head thrown back, her eyes closed. She was so stunning, she took his breath away.

"Like that, baby?"

At her deep moan, he had to gulp down hard to keep from driving into her with force. Descending one finger into her depths, he sighed against her lips. She was so ready, so moist for him. "Oh my my, you're going to feel too good."

"Abhinav." She closed her eyes and moaned as he leaned forward and caught her nipple in his mouth, his tongue stroking, his teeth tenderly biting. She moved her hips against his hand and he moaned, taking more of her breast into his mouth.

He slowly moved his finger in and out, stretching her as he went. His thumb circled her, increasing her suffering on purpose. He smiled against her lips, enjoying what he was doing to her and what she was doing to him.

Her hands fumbled with his zipper until he brushed them aside. "I want you, Trisha," he said against her lips.

His manhood sprang free from his pants and she gulped in air at the thought of him being buried deep inside her. She didn't have the chance to fool around as she'd wished. Abhinav grabbed her hips and lifted her onto his thick manhood. He teased her opening before gently pushing in deeper. Her eyes closed as he stretched and filled her and she braced her hands on his shoulders. With a pleasure filled moan she pushed down, taking him deeper.

"Fuck," Abhinav groaned as he grabbed her hips, holding her still.

"That's what I am doing." She growled against his neck, her tongue flicking out to lick his skin.

Slowly they began to move, her moans becoming lost in his hard kisses. Lifting her hips until he was almost out, she slowly slid back down his length. Abhinav groaned and settled his palms against her ribs, lifting her. "Again," he said and she obeyed.

Shots of liquid fire passed through Abhinav. Damn, she felt so hot. Hot and tight, like liquid lava enveloping him. Leaning forward, he pressed her wonderful breasts together and suckled both of them. He wanted to keep his mind off losing control. He wanted to feel her. Sliding his palm up the inside of her thigh, he found her puffed-up and brushed his thumb across it. She shuddered in his arms just as her inner walls shuddered along his manhood.

"Mmmm," he groaned. "I love that." He brushed his thumb across her again, applying just a little more force, and caught her gasp with his kiss. The muscles on the inside of her thighs began to shake as he continued with his teasing strokes against her.

"Abhinav," she moaned against his lips, the movement of her hips becoming more frantic.

"Come for me, baby." He applied more pressure to her, massaged it in minute circles, honing in on the one spot he knew would send her over the edge. She gasped and threw her head back. Her breasts thrust forward and he licked at one enlarged nipple, revelling in the tremble that passed through her. "That's it, baby. Come for me. Now."

She screamed as her release slammed through her and Abhinav grit his teeth, trying to hold his at bay. Her walls pulsed around him and he joined her with his own climax. She collapsed against him as he held her tight.

Sanjay was lying in the dingy prison cell looking at the ceiling of the four-walled room. He wondered how he had reached in such a bad state and cursed Trisha for his condition. He was desperate to get out of this mess, but all evidence seemed to be against him. There were many eye witnesses and it was difficult to get out of it easily. While he was lost in his thoughts, he heard the gate of his cell open up and a large shadow formed on the floor of his cell.

He turned around to see the guard staring at him.

"Yes, what do you want?" Sanjay asked impolitely.

"Someone is here to see you," the guard replied.

"And who would be that?" Sanjay got up from his bed and straightened up his prison uniform.

"It's the girl you raped."

"I did not rape anyone."

"You don't have to convince me, so save your energy for the court." The guard chuckled. "Come, let me take you to the visitor room and you can tell her that you didn't rape her." He smirked and pushed Sanjay ahead of him.

He looked at Sanjay's ass and said. "You have a fine ass. Just pray to God that you don't have to stay in this prison for long or someone will rape you too. Karma is a bitch you know!" The guard pressed his bamboo stick against Sanjay's ass.

Sanjay grunted but walked straight. He knew there was no point arguing with this guy. If there was anything that could be done, it would happen only by meeting the bitch Trisha.

Another guard opened up an iron door and Sanjay stepped into a room much similar to his cell, though larger in size. He could see a few wooden tables and chairs spread across in the room where other prisoners were talking to their visitors.

And the perfect Trisha came walking towards him. She was dressed perfectly in a youthful red Chanel suit with white satin cuffs, a matching top, and red and white shoes, holding out her hands as if she was an honoured guest.

The moment he saw Trisha, he was furious and ran towards her. He wanted to slap her, but the guard behind him hit a bamboo stick on his calves and he fell down. The pain that immediately began to swirl low in his calves only made him glare all the harder.

"You better behave or I will take you back to your cell." The guard looked at Sanjay, pointing his bamboo stick towards him.

Sanjay limped and sat down at the nearest chair. Trisha came and sat across him.

"How are you, my sweetheart?" Trisha tried to mock him.

Sanjay banged his fists on the table to control his anger. "Why have you come here? To ensure that I am rotting in hell? Don't worry. This is not over yet. I will get the best lawyers and get out of this prison. And then…"

"And then what?? You will come out and cheat many more people. How much is enough Sanjay? You have not been true to your business partner, to your wife and not even to me and even now you are giving me this godforsaken attitude!"

"There is nothing that I see can stop me from getting out, and when I do…"

"Well, then you haven't seen enough." Trisha bent down and got out her mobile and showed it to Sanjay. "Go ahead and play the video."

In the next few minutes, Sanjay's face turned from shades of red to completely white. He saw the video where Trisha was constantly saying 'no' and he was forcefully trying to make out with her.

"You fucking bitch!"

"Shhh…or the guard will come and hit you again baby. I can't see you in pain. So just be quiet and listen. That's the only way you can get out of here." She took back her mobile and kept it in her purse.

"I am waiting," replied Sanjay.

"You don't know what I have been through. Part of me would say, go fuck yourself you bastard!" She snapped.

"And what would the other part of you say?"

"The other part of me would say a hundred crore rupees as settlement amount to let you free."

Sanjay got furious and stood up from his seat. "You are a gold digging bitch."

"A hundred and twenty crores or maybe more then? What number would hurt you Sanjay, as much as you hurt me that night?" replied Trisha with tears in her eyes. Her acting was improving day by day.

"I am not giving you anything!" shouted Sanjay.

"Enough! You need to calm down," Trisha glared at Sanjay.

Sanjay thought about the whole situation. He was completely stuck. His lawyers could have handled the eye witnesses, but handling the video as evidence was impossible. He knew he was doomed. "I can offer you five crores. It's a good amount for you to enjoy your life."

"That's an insult. I discussed with my lawyer and he told me that the case is so strong that I will win it for sure. Do you want that to happen?"

"I am not going to give you my money!" Sanjay snapped.

"Your money? Excuse me, this money is not yours completely and you have stolen it from Abhinav. I am here to cut a deal for both of us or else my lawyer will make sure you stay here forever." His eyes were burning with anger, and Trisha continued, "I have enough eye witnesses to prove the rape. And this video is definitely the icing on the cake. Just think about it Sanjay. If you are free from this prison, then there is still chance that you can cheat more people and earn money, like you always do! Ok, I'll be a little kind to you. My final offer is seventy-five crores. "

"In your dreams!" replied Sanjay.

Sanjay though for a moment. The diamonds were worth a hundred crores. Even if he gave away half of the money, he would still have enough to lead a good life. It was important that he got out of the prison. "Fifty crores. You and Abhinav can divide it amongst yourselves the way you want. This is my final offer. Take it or leave it."

Trisha looked down and thought for a moment. "I will take it. But how will I get the money?"

"Well, I will sell some of my assets and in a day's time, you would get your money."

"What assets? The diamonds, eh!" smiled Trisha. "How will you sell diamonds worth crores bought from black money in a day?"

"That's none of your business, you bitch. You will get your share and that is what should be of concern to you."

"You know you can't sell the diamonds so soon and I need the money immediately or I will speak nothing but the truth in the court."

"Hold your leash for a day, Trisha. I will find a way to get you the money by tomorrow."

♦

In the cold stone jail visiting room, Sanjay sat behind the wooden table when Bharti came to meet him. She turned to face him and scrunched her nose in distaste. Their gazes remained locked in silent battle until Sanjay broke the spell.

"Thanks for coming Bharti. It means a lot to me!"

Bharti looked around as she moved her glares from her eyes to her head.

"Why have you called me here? Your lawyer kept begging me to come for just one last time. You have ruined my life, now what the hell do you want from me?" Bharti was furious.

"What? You really think I raped that girl?" asked Sanjay

She snorted. "Yeah, right!" She crossed her arms in front of her as she studied him through narrowed eyes. "How much more do you want to lie?"

He didn't say anything, just stared at her. His eyes darkened like gathering storm clouds, and a tremor ran through her.

"I think all you have been telling me are lies till now, Sanjay. I cannot trust anything but my judgment now," she glared at him.

"I am not lying Bharti. For once, I am not! Don't you get that?"

The prison guard by the barred door turned around and moved his beady eyes on Sanjay. Sanjay simmered down. He was silent for a moment, his eyes never leaving hers. "Ok, I am sorry. I didn't mean to shout at you. It's just that I am stuck in this rotten prison and…" Sanjay sighed.

The voice in Bharti's mind continued to remind her why she'd chosen to lead this life. She'd put everything she'd ever wanted on hold – a life, her career – all that forgotten for the sake of Sanjay.

If only she could make him go through the same pain. If only she could make him live a life of loneliness the way she had been living for the past few years.

With a resigned sigh, she tried to erase the negative thoughts from her mind and do what she came here to do. "I am not here to listen to your stories, Sanjay. I have heard enough of them. I came here to get the divorce papers signed."

Bharti threw a bunch of papers in front of him. He lifted up the papers in shock.

Sanjay studied her for a moment before answering.

"Why are you so surprised? Did you think I would let it go just like every other time in the past?"

He then looked back at Bharti. "I swear on God I didn't rape her. She is setting me up!" He inwardly groaned.

Bharti sighed, wondering if maybe she wasn't losing her mind, and returned her attention to her surroundings, desperate to try and keep her calm. "And why would she do that?"

He swallowed nervously, and then said, "I have not done anything bad to her. In fact…"

"Yes, in fact, you have been sleeping with her!"

"Bharti please…" he replied stubbornly.

"While sleeping with her is not as shameful a crime as raping her, it still is a crime in my eyes. You have ruined my life. You have broken my trust," said Bharti.

Bharti scowled and stood up. Sanjay knew Bharti's temper, and he was sure that she would leave if he continued to make her angry. And he didn't want that to happen. Putting his hand on Bharti's arm, he silently coaxed her to sit back down. "Bharti please listen to me!"

"No."

"Please. Just once."

"Fine," she growled as she sat back on the bench. "Say what you have to. But don't expect anything from me."

"I am innocent. I haven't raped her. The reason is that she is working for Abhinav Deo and he has set me up so that he can extract money from me and destroy me." He looked back down at the divorce papers to cover his anger.

"What? You don't have any money! You are in losses and covered in debts up to your nose. Are they out of their mind?" Bharti looked at her husband as if *he* had lost his mind.

"No, they aren't. Actually I haven't been completely honest with you."

"That I know!" Bharti narrowed her darkening eyes.

"No, there's more."

Bharti stared at him. "I can't believe I am having this conversation with you."

"Please. Listen. When I was working with Abhinav initially, he had started lobbying with clients and he wanted to move out of the partnership and eat away all the profits."

"So?"

"So I embezzled funds slowly and converted them into diamonds over the last few years before the split happened."

"Sanjay, I am not sure if I even know you. I have been living with you but I am not sure who you are? A fraudster? A lecherous husband? Or an unethical employer who uses his models by promising them larger roles in advertisements?"

"I am the same Sanjay you fell in love with Bharti. Yes, I stole some money, but it was for our better future. I knew Abhinav had wrong intentions since the beginning and he was just using me. I had to be secure."

"Ok, so why are you telling me all this? How is it relevant? I don't want your money. I want nothing from you except your signatures on these divorce documents." She eyed the documents on the table.

"Bharti I will sign wherever you want to. But first you have to help me. For one last time."

"And that is?"

"Abhinav and Trisha are now blackmailing me."

"What?"

"Trisha had come to prison today. She has asked me for a huge sum of money to settle this out of court or else she has threatened to press charges and prove me guilty."

"Won't your lawyers take you out of this mess?"

"I have discussed with them."

"And what did they say?"

"They said that I have very little chance of winning this case. There were many people in the party and most of them would say the same story as what you believed was true. So mostly I will be held guilty for rape."

Bharti sat thinking for a minute. "How much money do you need to give her?"

"I need to give her fifty crores."

Bharti's eyes opened wider in shock, but she calmed herself a bit to ask, "What is the worth of the diamonds?"

He looked down at his hands as though thinking. "A little over a hundred crores."

She shook her head as she stared at him warily. "Are you serious? That's a lot of money, Sanjay."

"I know. It's all I got."

"What do you want me to do?"

"I want you to go home and open my black closet."

"Ok," Bharti sighed and nodded her head.

"When you open the drawer on the right and move your hand on the top inside surface, you would realize that I have pasted a key there."

"You are such an ass." She scowled.

"Please listen."

"What's the key for?" She narrowed her eyes.

"That is the key to my locker in SCHC Bank."

Bharti raised an eyebrow. "Ok."

"You will have to go to the bank branch and use this key for locker no 764 and take the diamonds from there. Once you have the diamonds, just call Abhinav and ask him to meet you along with Trisha."

"What if they take the diamonds and still don't keep their promise."

"Don't worry. That is something I have figured out. My lawyers will give you a statement which would clearly mention that Trisha has decided to take off the case and not press charges."

"You need to get that document signed from her before you give away the diamonds."

"Ok. Sounds good. But this doesn't change anything between us."

"What do you mean?"

"I am still going to divorce you. I am doing this last thing for you Sanjay. And once I do it, I need your signatures on these papers and independence from your life."

"Please help me out of the prison and I will sign wherever you want."

Bharti stepped out of the prison and called on the lawyer's number that Sanjay had given her. Even if this was the last thing she had to do for Sanjay, for her independence, she was ready to do it.

"Hello, Mr. Harish. This is Bharti Kapoor. Sanjay Kapoor's wife." The words slashed her like a blade. That is what she had been all her life – Sanjay Kapoor's wife! And she had no identity of her own.

"Hello Mrs. Kapoor! How can I help you?"

"Actually, I just stepped out of the prison after meeting Sanjay. He mentioned that you are going to give me some papers on which I need to take Trisha's signature."

"Well, the papers are ready. But do you think that girl is going to sign these? It looks unlikely as it gives a clean chit to Sanjay."

"Well, you leave that to me. I will try to get it done."

"If you say so. Tell me where should I send the papers?"

"I am going home and you can send someone with the papers. Hope you have our home address."

"Oh yes, of course. Sanjay is an old client of our firm and we have all the records. Please don't worry, I will send someone with the papers in the next one hour.

She parked her car in the driveway of her home and rushed to unlock the door. She locked the door behind her and looked around her house. Bharti stood inside the door and felt the worry lines deepen around her eyes. She rushed to Sanjay's closet and unlocked it. She opened the right drawer and sat on the floor. She moved her hand on the upper inner surface of the drawer just as Sanjay had asked her to. Her expression changed as her fingers went over a slippery surface. Probably it was a cello tape and it held the keys to hundreds of crores. She used her other hand to rip the tape off.

There it was! The key to Sanjay's freedom.

Bharti wondered how less she knew her husband. All this while he had been cheating on her, even keeping secrets about the money he had and making her believe that he was under heavy debts.

She came and sat on the bed with the key on her palm. The etched letters SCHC 764 were shining in the overhead lights. She picked up her purse and carefully dropped the key into a small pocket and closed the zipper. She checked her watch. She still had time to go to the bank and retrieve the diamonds.

Bharti walked to the kitchen and poured herself a glass of water. This was getting really complicated. Diamonds! Money! Prison!

Her throat was parched. So she picked up the water bottle from the table and poured some for herself. Wrapping both hands around the glass, she took a sip. She turned around and walked towards one of the many chairs around the dining table. Pulling out a chair, she sat down, setting the bottle on the table in front of her.

The doorbell rang.

Bharti froze at the sound of it.

Who could it be? Did someone else know about the diamonds? Or had Trisha sent someone to steal away the key? Such thoughts wandered in her mind as she walked slowly towards the door.

The bell rang again, sending a chill down her spine.

She summed up her courage and looked through the peep hole.

There was a young guy standing in front of her.

She tried to speak at the top of her voice. "Who is it?"

"Ma'am, I have come with the papers."

"What papers? I haven't asked for anything!" she blurted.

"Ma'am you can talk to your lawyer. He has sent me. I work in his law firm. He asked me to give these papers to you."

Bharti took a deep breath and reached out for the door lock and unlocked it.

She studied the young boy with a frown. He stood just outside the door, one hand on the door frame, the other holding a brown packet. He was wearing a pair of beige pants and dark chocolate coloured shirt.

She took the papers from the boy and he tilted his head to the side, studying her as he crossed his arms over his chest.

"Thank you." She quickly locked the door even before listening to his reply and sighed with relief. She went back and picked up her purse to check if the key was still in the pocket. It was.

She took her purse and the papers and walked outside her house. She wasn't aware of the bank's location, so she fed details of the address on the maps application in her phone, and zoomed towards it. Her heart was thumping out so loud that she could hear it over the bass of her car stereo.

She saw the SCHC bank on her left side. It stood majestically across a large step of stairs. Bharti hurriedly climbed up the stairs, periodically checking if she had the key. After all, the key was worth crores.

Bharti entered the bank. The lights were bright and two of the three tellers behind the counters smiled at her and then continued their work. She looked around for the manager's desk and found it at the far right corner.

"Hello ma'am, how can I help you?" the manager across the desk asked her.

"Well, I have a security deposit locker here and I need to get some stuff out of it."

"Sure ma'am, let me just check the records."

"The locker is in the name of my husband Mr. Sanjay Kapoor."

"Sure, I will just search the database. Please give me a minute." He typed the name on the keyboard and looked at the screen in front of him.

Bharti wiped her hands on the sides of her trousers. Her hands were sweaty with the cold key tightly gripped in her hand.

"Well yes, you are right. He does have a locker here and it shows you as a nominee in the account. If you don't mind, can I see some identification proof?"

"Sure!" Bharti dug out her driving license and handed it over to him.

"Thanks, this is fine."

"Now if you would please take me to the locker. I've got things to do," Bharti said.

The manager eyed her suspiciously but then forced a smile. "Certainly, Mrs. Kapoor. Please come this way." He waived his hand towards a metal gate.

Bharti had seen such a setting usually in the movies. A guard was standing at the gate and he wished her good morning as they entered the gate. The locker room looked like a large chocolate with brown coloured lockers connected neatly one on top of the other. The manager searched for locker number 746, and guided her towards it.

"Ma'am, we need to insert the two keys together and unlock the locker."

Both Bharti and the manager inserted the keys and the locker opened. The manager smiled at her, pulled out a large box and placed it on the table in the centre of the room.

"I will let you have a look at the contents of the drawer in private while I wait outside."

Bharti nodded to him and he turned around and walked out of the door.

Bharti opened the box and found a black velvet sack in it. She untied the knot on the velvet case and poured out the contents on her hand. The diamonds came rushing out onto her palms. A perfect rainbow was trapped inside the flawless diamonds. The stunning beauty of the stones could only be matched by the breathtaking beauty of the woman who was admiring them. Bharti's cream skin was dappled in the cornucopia of colours emanating from the diamonds.

Bharti, tears welling in her eyes, carefully put back the diamonds into the velvet sack and tied the knot carefully before keeping the diamonds in her bag.

She placed the box back into the locker and called back the manager to help her lock the same.

Bharti had the diamonds with her and she knew what she was going to do with them. She had already planned this with Ankit. He worked in a jewellery store and had figured out a great contact to sell the diamonds.

She lifted her phone and dialled in. "I have the diamonds. The plan worked! And what's more... they are worth a hundred crores!"

"What! That's a hell lot of money. You never told me it was such a big amount."

"Ankit , even I wasn't aware of it. But now we have them! And that's all that matters. But where the hell are you? You were supposed to be here. We shouldn't be talking about this on the phone!

"I am just about to reach! Look on your right."

As she looked on her right, she saw Ankit walking out of a taxi. He came running towards her and lifted her in his arms.

She looked him in the eye. "This plan isn't over until we have sold these. I have done my part of the deal. Now it's your turn."

Ankit chickened out a bit. "Sweetheart, these diamonds are really a hell lot more expensive than what I had thought. Are you sure you want to steal so much money?"

"Steal? Excuse me! Are you out of your mind? This is my money. My father invested in the company so it's rightfully mine and not Sanjay's. You need to understand darling that this is the only way we can have a great life. Together."

Bharti had no intention of letting him go anywhere. She was just using him since the day she realized he was working in a jeweller's shop and could come in handy to exchange the diamonds for money. She smiled up at him, her lips parting in invitation. She put her other hand on his shoulder and kissed him lightly on the corner of his mouth.

With her so close to him and the love holding them together, he stopped thinking about the risk of selling the diamonds and abandoned himself to her feel, warmth and passion.

♦

He looked incredible with his hair parted on the side. The black jeans contoured to his waist and hips, and the black shirt stretched across his wide chest.

He rubbed his palms up and down his arms in an attempt to remove the goosebumps that he felt because of the cash lying in his room. She had convinced him to make the sale. But it was not an easy one. Such sales were common in the jeweller's trade, but never at such a large amount. So he had divided the quantity into two and dealt with two different guys. The whole process had taken some time, but he was happy that now he could take the cash and live with his love forever.

Although he appeared relaxed as he strolled over to the car, there was tenseness about him as he constantly scanned the streets around him. His eyes never seemed to stay in one place for too long. It was as though he were watching for something…or someone. He carefully placed the bags of cash in the trunk and locked it.

He bit his lower lip as he stepped into the car and took his seat. He felt a bit nervous today. The force of the sudden start of the ignition threw him back as he pressed the accelerator. He tried concentrating on the drive as the car sped, and tried to fight against the nausea that threatened. He had to get away from this nervousness.

He stopped at a red light, glanced into the rear-view mirror to see if he was being followed, then turned right on to the road which would lead him to love and happiness.

◆

Going over to the basin, she looked at her reflection in the mirror and blinked. Dear god, her cheeks were looking deep red. She couldn't go out looking like this. Grabbing a hand towel, she moistened it with cool water and pressed it to her cheeks.

She leaned back against the basin and tried to compose herself. It did no good.

She actually felt a little heavy headed from the situation she was in. She was worried if they would be able to leave the city before anyone got suspicious and informed the police about their plan. It took a few minutes for her to get herself together and go outside.

It was hard to believe that a few minutes ago, Ankit had told her that he had sold the diamonds and the money was now with him. He was coming to get her and then they could leave the city. The knowledge of what was going to happen later was in the back of her mind the whole time and it was making her worried as hell. She could hardly wait to reach the place where Ankit had asked her to come.

Her head throbbed and she no longer wanted to think about it. Her heart thumped as she prepared for the evening ahead. With haste and enthusiasm she rummaged through the already packed clothes in her suitcases for something suitable to wear. Mentally, she discarded many dresses before choosing a sundress of embroidered cotton, hoping this would brighten her day.

She swallowed hard. What the heck was going to happen?

As she reached the agreed spot, she looked at her watch. She had reached on time, but he had still not reached. She got worried.

She fiddled with her phone to check if the address that he had messaged to her was correct.

She heard the coughing of an engine as a car rumbled over the road. She turned around and saw the sedan directly behind her slow and turn down the cemented road toward her. The front door opened and he emerged from the car, clean-shaven and hair still damp from the shower.

"Trisha!"

"Ankit!" She rushed to him and held him tightly in her arms. Her arm slowly tightened around his waist. As she drew him into her, her eyes never wavered from his. There was an unspoken victory in them, as if he they were congratulating her for what they had planned together.

Yes, Trisha and Ankit had planned it all.

He took her mouth slowly, gently, barely grazing her lips at first. Her mind was spinning, and she clung to his shoulders for support. His strength, the sheer power of his rugged masculinity enticed her to surrender to the crazy swirl of emotions spinning through her. Inexplicably, she eased her hold and moved away. "We don't have much time. It's time to go."

"You are right!"

"Have you got the cash?" she asked.

"Yes," replied Ankit as he held Trisha's hand and literally pulled her to the car to show her the large bags.

Trisha jumped up in excitement. She opened the zipper of one bag and found it full of currency notes. "That's a hell lot of money!" She exclaimed.

"It sure is." He replied with a broad grin on his face.

"Cheers to a great life ahead!"

Trisha looked at Ankit as they gave each other a high five.

Trisha and Ankit had done it just the way they had planned it. And now they were rich as hell.

Epilogue

Trisha and Ankit had always been impeccable with their planning, and this one was no exception. They were a great team.

They were fast running out of money from the previous adventure about a year back and that's when they decided to pull the next one. Where could they get loads of money? Perhaps the underworld! Too dangerous. Bollywood? Maybe. Advertising!! Juicy, yet safer.

Basis their research of top fifty couples in the advertising industry, they had shortlisted Sanjay and Bharti, because their marriage was a sham. And it was visible to anyone who cared to dig slightly deeper that neither of them were true to each other. While Sanjay was busy filling the hollowness of his life in the arms of young models, Bharti was busy trying to keep herself busy in shopping by gaining momentary happiness through materialistic pleasures.

So that is how Trisha and Ankit decided to enter the couple's life.

Trisha bumped into Sanjay in a pub, spilling his drink on him. Knowing his lecherous nature of sleeping around with models despite being married, it was easy to lure him into a web of lust and deception. She had seduced him into having raw forceful sex over time and fulfilled all his fantasies till the day he was completely under her sway. She toiled much with him, although she hated how his brain worked from his balls. But despite all that, the plan wasn't reaching anywhere, for though Sanjay kept referring to the diamonds, he never revealed their location.

So they had no option but to corner him to a situation where he was helpless. Over and over, Trisha played sex games with him in which she refused to have sex and Sanjay forced her into it. Soon that became a big fantasy for him and finally she could trap him on the day of the party by posing it as a rape.

On the other hand, Ankit followed Bharti for over a month to understand her routine. The best way to enter her life was when she went out for her favourite pastime – shopping. So that's what he did. He paid off three guys to run across the mall's entrance to bump into Bharti forcefully. That's when he got the chance to come into her life, acting as the knight in shining armour, a chivalrous, sexy man. He knew Bharti held strong the façade of being the victim, but she was as eager to satisfy her lust outside of her marriage as Sanjay.

Bharti was no fool, and had her eyes and ears open at all times. She knew about Sanjay's escapades long before even his closest confidants got a whiff of it. Being the strong woman that she was, she could have left Sanjay a long time ago. But she couldn't do that because she was habitual of extravagant shopping and the life of the rich and famous.

Bharti always wanted to get back at her husband for sleeping around with random girls, and not her. The moment she found out that Ankit had contacts within the jeweller's trade, she made sure she could use him to sell off the diamonds. The sex only came as one of the perks.

The rivalry between Abhinav and Sanjay had just been the icing on the cake. Trisha and Ankit ended up dragging Abhinav into the plan knowingly. Trisha used Abhinav, for she knew that Sanjay was jealous of Abhinav and this helped in pushing Sanjay further to the corner. So while Abhinav believed that he was using Trisha to plot against Sanjay, it was, in reality, exactly the opposite.

Bharti kept waiting for Ankit to come over with the money. She didn't want to share the wealth with anyone, and she could have used Ankit to fulfil her desires till someone better came by. But he never turned up on the assigned day with the cash or the diamonds. He had suddenly vanished. She realised she had made a huge mistake by putting even that little bit of trust in Ankit. She should have been more careful, but it was too late now. She thought of reporting it to the police, but she knew well that the diamonds had been bought from black money, and she would have had no answers to give to the police.

Bharti wanted revenge and Sanjay's money to live an extravagant life. Though she lost out on the money, she could not have let this spoil the fun for her. Since Trisha's statement never came, Bharti never bothered about pulling Sanjay out of his doom.

With Sanjay behind bars, she had to look for someone who could afford her. And real soon. How about Abhinav, she wondered! After all, enemy's enemy is usually a friend.

She was lost in thoughts after downing quite a bit of gin when her iPhone buzzed. He eyes were hazy but she managed to read the name. Ankit. That bastard! She hastily pulled the phone towards her and slurred a hello into the mouthpiece.

"I hope you didn't wait for me too long, my love! I knew we were to be together for this lifetime, but then...sudden change in plans!"

Bharti could barely speak. She was struggling for words.

"I hope you're not drowning yourself in alcohol to forget me." He had a strange devilish charm in his voice even now.

"You bastard! I will..."

"Yes, honey. I will miss you too." He rubbed some more salt on her wounds. "I was just about to take off forever and thought of saying thank you. It's always fun to work with a sexy ass who thinks she is a smart-ass!" He chuckled.

"You will pay for this, Ankit. I have never seen a man filthier than you," Bharti spat into the phone.

Before he hung up, he said in his husky voice, "*The pleasure is all mine.*"